THE MYSTERY OF THE DEBONAIR DUKE

REMINGTONS OF THE REGENCY BOOK 1

ELLIE ST. CLAIR

Facebook: Ellie St. Clair

Cover by AJF Designs

Do you love historical romance? Receive access to a free ebook, as well as exclusive content such as giveaways, contests, freebies and advance notice of pre-orders through my mailing list!

Sign up here!

The Remingtons of the Regency
The Mystery of the Debonair Duke
The Secret of the Dashing Detective
The Clue of the Brilliant Bastard
The Quest of the Reclusive Rogue

For a full list of all of Ellie's books, please see
www.elliestclair.com/books.

CHAPTER 1

*G*iles felt his father's eyes judging him as he took a seat behind the desk that didn't seem to belong to him any more than the rest of the furnishings in the house did.

Even in death, his father made sure that Giles would always know the wrath of that disapproving stare.

Giles promised himself to soon rid the room of the portrait. It would be one more step forward, allowing them all to fly free from beneath the burden his father had kept them under.

Although the women of the house seemed to have already released their wings. While Giles was the duke by the same name his father had been, upon the demise of the previous duke just over a year ago, his mother, grandmother, and sisters had asserted themselves as though Giles had no say whatsoever.

Which he supposed he didn't.

The ledgers sat untouched on the monstrosity of a heavy walnut desk before him. The entries, he knew, would be neat, meticulous, perfect — just like everything else in his father's life.

With one exception — his son. His only son, and the one who, despite his utmost chagrin, inherited everything. Including the title and responsibility that Giles had no wish for. He and his father had parted ways long ago, and as much as Giles was pleased he had avoided more time with the man, he was beginning to wish that he had, at the very least, learned a bit more about the responsibilities of running a dukedom. Part of him wondered if he should run the whole thing into the ground, just to spite his father's ghost.

"Giles! Are you in there?"

His mother's knock on the door reminded him of why he would never do so. He could have easily done it to his father, but never to his mother nor his sisters.

"Come in," he called back.

She stepped in the doorway but stopped short, her eyes widening as she looked around the heavy masculine room; one that, as far as Giles was aware, had been off limits to any woman for years now.

"What in heavens name are you doing, sitting here in the dark?"

He hadn't lit a candle, the fire was in embers, and the heavy navy curtains that covered the window but for the small crack between them prevented much light from entering. His father's portrait above the fireplace across from him was hung upon hunter green walls, while its gilded frame matched those that covered the rest of the room. The large, mustard yellow chairs across from the desk made it nearly impossible to walk across the room unencumbered.

"I am… pondering."

"Right. Yes," she said with a bemused expression on her still-beautiful face. Her green eyes, under her auburn hair, glinted at him. "I do hope you are considering which of the women who will be in attendance tonight you might take an interest in."

Giles groaned as he leaned forward, one hand running through his hair which he insisted on leaving about an inch too long for the current fashion. "Mother, you know I wish that you were not holding this ball tonight. I have no desire to wed, at least, not anytime soon, and I—"

"Giles," she said with that patience she had always possessed, patience that had not passed down to him. "You are the duke now. And as duke, you have certain responsibilities. Responsibilities that include producing heirs."

"Elizabeth, you really should allow the young man to take a breath as duke before you go shoving young self-important women into his arms."

A true, wide grin sprang to Giles' face at his grandmother's voice in the corridor, even as his mother shut her eyes and took a deep breath. He loved his straightforward grandmother as much as she had a soft spot for him in her crotchety old heart.

His mother, ever the proper duchess, straightened her spine as her mother joined her in the doorway. Lady Winchester may now walk with a cane in hand, but she held herself as regally as any queen.

"He is not so young anymore. And I hardly think, Mother, that a lack of women is an issue for Giles," she said.

The sentiment had Giles standing up and gasping, "Mother!"

"The issue," she continued as if Giles wasn't even there, "is finding the *right* woman for him."

"And you have just the one, I assume?" Giles' grandmother asked with a twinkle in her eye.

"I do," his mother said with a determined tilt of her chin. "Lady Maria."

"Lady Maria Bennington?" Giles confirmed, his tone grim.

"Just the one," his mother said with a triumphant smile. "I do hope you remember her."

"I do, but Mother, she's… she's…" He struggled to find the right word to describe her, one that would be accurate and yet polite.

"She's a bore," his grandmother finished for him, and Giles nodded in thanks.

"Exactly."

"A *bore* is exactly the woman you need to help you manage your new responsibilities," his mother said, holding her nose up a slight inch higher. "Responsibilities, might I remind you, that you have neglected for nearly a year. You need a woman who understands how to manage not just one household, but multiple estates. Who has been raised for such a role and who will welcome it. Who can oversee your sisters—"

Giles managed to smother his laugh with a cough, but his grandmother had no problem letting out a snort.

"If you find someone to control those girls, then I will take her on myself!" his grandmother said. "They were running around unchecked long before Warwick died. He just never noticed."

"Mother," his own mother began, but before an argument could begin, Giles walked over and placed a hand on the small of each of their backs as he led them out of the cold study and into the corridor beyond.

"Let us see how the preparations are coming along, shall we?" he asked, which seemed to humor them, although Giles didn't miss the shrewd look his grandmother sent his way.

"You know," his mother said as they approached the ball-room, "no one ever said you couldn't continue to live the life you currently lead. Just because you'll have a wife won't mean—"

"For goodness' sake, Elizabeth, the man is a loveable rogue, not an adulterer!" his grandmother cut in.

Giles only sighed, shaking his head, but when they stepped into the ballroom the argument dissipated as they took in all that was before him. The ballroom itself was always resplendent, but with the columns decorated and more greenery than a Vauxhall Gardens strung throughout, it was more magnificent than the set of a Shakespeare play.

"Oh, heavens," his grandmother said. "This is extravagant."

His mother, well aware of what was awaiting her as she had organized it all, looked around in satisfaction. "It's perfect. Exactly what we need. It has been so long since we have had any type of celebration here," she said wistfully.

Which was true. His father hadn't allowed anything of the sort, not one to welcome guests in his home. Not that Giles would have attended, anyway. As soon as he had started school, he had stayed at Eton or with a friend for the holidays. His father's death had been the only event to bring him back to Warwick House.

"You should wear red, Juliana. It complements your hair."

Giles tilted his head at the voices arriving from down the hall. It seemed that his sisters were of a similar mind.

"Red? But Pru, do you really think—? Mother!"

Juliana and Prudence wore matching smiles of innocence as they approached, and Giles struggled to hide his grin. They had been vexing his mother for the entirety of their lives, and it seemed now that they were on the marriage mart, he was included in the list of people they were convinced impeded them from the happiness they felt that they deserved.

"You most certainly will *not* be wearing red!" his mother

exclaimed as she ran her eyes over her daughters. "You will be wearing the white that I selected for you."

"Oh, Mother, white is so dull," Juliana said, doing nothing to hide her grimace. "Would you settle for blue?"

His mother considered for a moment. Despite the stiff formality that she attempted to present to everyone in her acquaintance, at the end of the day, she loved her children more than anything else.

"Very well. The pale blue that Madame Blanchet recently finished. That will do nicely."

"Wonderful," Juliana beamed, her smile one that Giles was sure would be breaking many hearts this season. He had an inkling that this entire conversation had been contrived to end with his mother's acquiescence on the blue dress.

"Prudence, what have you chosen?" his mother asked with an eyebrow raised. While Juliana could charm the vilest of hearts, Prudence was much more straightforward — very like their grandmother, if Giles was being honest, not that anyone would likely consider comparison to the formidable Lady Winchester to be a compliment. It had, however, meant that Prudence had scared off — selectively or by accident — most gentlemen who had thus far considered her as a wife.

"I shall wear the pink," she said decidedly, which their mother approved with a nod.

"Very well. Off you go, then. Our guests will be arriving in just a few hours."

They nodded, although Juliana hesitated, shifting from one foot to the other.

"Mother…" she began, clearing her throat, and her mother raised a brow.

"Yes?"

"Now that we are out of mourning… well, the thing is, people are going to talk, you know."

"Talk about what?"

Their mother far preferred to pretend that nothing unto-ward ever occurred, to live as though the world was all as perfect as she wished it to be. It was one of the few things that she and her husband had in common — the ability to wipe their hands of whatever it was that didn't serve them.

"About Father's death," Prudence said much more bluntly. "People have questions. As do we, for we know nothing more than anyone else."

Giles and his mother exchanged a glance.

"Tell them all the truth," Giles suggested, leaning against the doorframe as the servants bustled within, putting the finishing touches on turning the ballroom into some kind of Grecian fantasy. "That we do not know the details of what happened to him but hope to find out soon."

"Absolutely not!" his mother hissed, rounding on him. "You know what we are to say. That he had apoplexy and died."

"Well, someone out there knows that is a lie."

"I hardly think they will be coming forward anytime soon," snapped his mother.

"Father was poisoned," Giles said, raising a brow. "There are already rumors. You know how people are. As much as we try to contain the story, servants talk. Physicians talk. People will know. If we try to cover it up, it is going to look like we did it ourselves."

"Giles!" His mother covered her heart with her hand.

Prudence looked rather ill at ease. "The thing is, Giles…" she said, biting her lip, "people are already saying that."

Giles straightened. Of course, he was well aware of what the talk was. Who wouldn't suspect the son who had hated his father, and who'd inherited everything from the man? He had more to gain by his father's death than anyone in the entire world, and everyone knew of their falling out. What they didn't realize, however, was that he could have spent years without assuming the title and been perfectly happy.

"They can say what they want," he said dismissively. "I don't particularly care. In case all of you have forgotten, I am the Duke of Warwick and I hardly think anyone is going to be coming forward and accusing me of anything, now, are they?"

His mother wrung her hands nervously while his grandmother eyed him with, if he wasn't mistaken, a touch of approval. His sisters seemed quite riveted by his reaction.

"If it helps," he finally continued, "I have hired a man to look into his death. I figured that, even if he doesn't find anything, it will make it appear that we have questions about our father's death."

"Do you think he will find anything?" Juliana asked, leaning forward, her eyes shining with intrigue.

Giles shrugged. "I don't know, and I don't particularly care. For, do you want to know the truth? I am glad he's dead."

CHAPTER 2

*G*iles surveyed the ballroom that seemed to be bursting at the seams. It was awash in spinning color and an array of perfumes, all which threatened to make him sick. He dutifully stood beside his mother while she spoke with Lady Hemingway, who had been accompanied tonight by her son. Lady Hemingway had been married to the previous Duke of Warwick's cousin and had been the one family member to whom his mother had always been particularly close, even after she decided she no longer wanted anything to do with the duke outside of societal responsibilities. Giles' father hadn't had any siblings, and his second cousin had always been more of a brother to him than any other man.

Giles remembered the man from when he was a child. Lord Hemingway had been grown from the same seed as his father had been, meaning that Giles had kept as much space between him and the man as possible. He remembered one particular incident that involved a practical joke and a belt. From that day forward, he had kept himself scarce when the earl was around.

The current Lord Hemingway, on the other hand, was not that bad of a chap, and he seemed as affable today as he had always been.

"How long has it been since your father died?" he asked his cousin.

"About three years now," Hemingway replied. His hair was a sandy brown, his eyes serious, but his smile pleasant enough. Giles wasn't sure he was the type of man he would invite for a drink at his club, but he would certainly sit down with him if he happened to see him there.

"How have you found it?" Giles asked nonchalantly. "Filling his shoes, that is."

Hemingway tilted his head at him, his brow furrowed. "It's been as expected. These are our lives. We were raised to take their places."

"Of course," Giles said, nodding as he took a sip of the bourbon he held in his hand, gripping it tightly. He didn't particularly enjoy events such as these — where he was supposed to act in an expected manner, speak of proper subjects, dance with approved women — but, like Hemingway said, he had been raised to function at them.

Hemingway seemed to sense his unease, for he leaned in closer. "Every other man out there would kill to be in our shoes. We are privileged, Warwick. Might as well enjoy it — as it seems you have been?"

He nudged him with an elbow and winked, and Giles managed a weak smile. He knew he had earned quite the reputation, although he wasn't sure he deserved as much of it as he was given.

"Speaking of..." Hemingway said, his voice trailing off as he stepped backward when their mothers turned around to them with matching smiles of eagerness.

They were not, however, alone.

"Lady Maria," he said, forcing the polite smile on his face

when he saw who was in their company. "It is lovely to see you."

"Isn't it?" his mother practically beamed.

"Have you met Lord Hemingway?" Giles said, forcing his cousin to step back into the circle.

"I have had the pleasure of meeting his mother," Lady Maria said, a gracious smile on her face. She was the picture of a perfect young lady tonight. Her blond hair was artfully arranged away from her face, her crystal blues eyes shining, her cheeks pink. Giles found himself wondering if she had been born with such a complexion or if she had done something to make it so. "If Lord Hemingway is nearly as pleasant as his mother, then I am most grateful to meet him."

The woman said all the right things. She was everything he knew he should want. Everything he needed, as far as his mother was concerned, a fact that she was obviously trying to make him aware of when she shot him such pointed glances that he wondered how the entirety of the ballroom didn't notice.

"Do you hear that?" his mother said. "The musicians are beginning again."

Giles gritted his teeth. It wasn't that he didn't enjoy dancing, or conversation with lovely young women. It was that he despised situations in which he could not be himself. Well, he would do his best to charm the young woman, play the role his mother required.

Then he would make his escape.

* * *

"Can you believe the number of people that have filled our ballroom?" Juliana asked, her eyes wide as she stared at the magnificence of the colors before her.

"I do believe it," Emma replied with a nod. "Your mother

should have just written on the invitation that this event is being held to select a wife for your brother. The fact that the duke is young, handsome, and charming? It's like waving a honeypot in front of a swarm of flies."

"Well, when you put it so eloquently, it is hard to believe that anyone could resist," Juliana said, laughing. "Except you, of course."

Emma tilted her head. "I know far too much about your brother to want him for a husband, I'm afraid."

She watched the man now, gracefully moving about the dance floor, his partner the perfect princess that was Lady Maria Bennington. It was not that Emma had anything against Lady Maria. In fact, she actually quite liked the woman. But it was hard not to feel a slight bit of jealousy when she was everything Emma knew she herself should be and yet everything she was not.

"Giles was not particularly pleased about this event," Prudence remarked from beside Juliana. Emma and Juliana were the closest of friends since they had been young girls and Emma had practically grown up with the family. While everyone on the outside assumed that the Remington family was the apple of the *ton's* eye, the truth was that the relationships within the family had been like an apple filled with worms. Most had stemmed from the previous duke, and while Juliana and Prudence had spent the past year in mourning, they had already stepped out from under the man's giant, frigid shadow.

"Why would he not be?" Emma asked, perplexed. As much as she despised everything the rakish man stood for — a rakish man who had abandoned his family when they needed him the most — she couldn't help but appreciate the way the fabric of his breeches stretched over his thighs as he stepped past them, nor the broadness of his shoulders beneath the finest of black linen jackets. While Juliana and

Prudence both had the coloring of their mother with rich auburn hair and green eyes, Giles' hair was as black as night, his eyes a bright blue that could pierce through one's soul.

And then, of course, there was that devastating smile. The one that had charmed half the *ton* — the female half.

But not her, Emma reminded herself. She knew him far too well — even if he barely acknowledged her presence — and she could never admire a man who would use women as he did.

Even if he was a duke. A duke that she should never think of as *Giles*, but she couldn't help it, not when that was how his sisters had referred to him all of their lives, for Giles and his father had been in agreement that Giles would not use any of the courtesy titles.

"Never thought you would be the type to throw yourself at my grandson."

Emma jumped with a start. She had forgotten that Lady Winchester was standing to her other side.

"I'm not at all, actually," she said, before hastily adding, "not that he wouldn't make the most agreeable husband, of course."

The woman's lips turned up in what Emma considered was perhaps a grin, or an amused smile at least, and it was Emma's turn to be curious.

"Forgive my impertinence, Lady Winchester, but why would you think I want anything different than the other young ladies who fill this ballroom?" She couldn't help but ask, looking furtively behind her to see if Juliana and Prudence were listening, but they were whispering to one another as they also watched Giles — who was now twirling Lady Maria around with more elegance and charm than one man should possess.

"Because you have a head on your shoulders," Lady Winchester said before tilting her head back ever so slightly

ELLIE ST. CLAIR

and releasing a laugh that was enough to turn the heads of her granddaughters. "You would never fall for his charming words of seduction nor the honeyed smiles. You, my dear, would want more than a man who can only give you half of himself. But it's his loss, for I find you quite clever."

"Most would say that I am far too observant for my own good," Emma murmured. Just this morning she had heard her father grumbling to his man-of-business that he was soon going to have to do something about her, being still unmarried despite the few half-hearted offers she had received.

It wasn't that she didn't appreciate them. It was just that she had no wish to spend her life in a relationship with a man who treated her like another one of his employees — even if she would be a well-kept one. That had been the relationship she had known, growing up watching her parents, the Earl and Countess of Kilmingham. Then one day her mother seemed to have enough of pretending and retreated to her bedroom from where she hardly ever emerged. Emma was aware that she had succumbed to the weight of her life and an illness that seemed to be of her mind and not her body, but there didn't appear to be anything she could do about it.

Except learn from her parents' mistakes — and the right decisions made by Bernard and Lily, who had shown her that there was another way — a marriage full of love and devotion to one another.

They may be servants in her house — gardener and cook — but it was obviously possible to be happy no matter one's station, if that life was spent with the right person.

She had never told another person how passionately she wanted the same. She assumed she would be laughed at for thinking such a thing, told that she didn't have the choice.

"Has she mentioned, Grandmother, that she doesn't seem

14

to have a desire for *any* man?" Juliana rather unhelpfully chimed in, her green eyes dancing as she teased Emma. "Emma finds them all too dull or stupid."

"Juliana!" Emma exclaimed, her eyes widening on her friend in horror. What Juliana said was true, but it was hardly something to be repeated, most especially to a countess.

Fortunately, Lady Winchester only laughed. "Most are, my dear. Most are," she said, patting her hand. "Just remember, it's not about finding a man to match you in every way. It's about finding a man to *fit* you in each way."

The three young women stared after Lady Winchester as she walked across the room with more dignity than any other woman in the ballroom, with or without a cane, which she was now using to bat away a piece of ivy that had fallen from one of the marble pillars and threatened to hamper her path.

"I do wish I can be something like your grandmother when I grow up," Emma said with a chuckle.

"I am glad you are not insulted," Juliana said. "She does mean well."

"She doesn't," Emma said, still laughing. "But I enjoy her."

"It is true what I said," Juliana continued. "Besides, we all know you would rather be elbows deep in dirt in your garden than standing in this ballroom."

Juliana was right. Emma was already excitedly thinking about the small patch of strawberries she was going to plant, wondering how she could possibly make a hybrid out of the fruit.

Emma ignored her and returned to their previous conversation.

"What I am truly looking for is love. Is that really too much to ask?"

Juliana and Prudence exchanged a glance before Juliana

shrugged her shoulders. "I am not sure that we are the best people to answer such a question," she said, to which Emma nodded.

"Of course. I'm sorry."

"Don't be," Juliana said with a wave of her hand. "I have decided that I am going to marry a man who can keep me in all the habits that I currently enjoy. A man with wealth and a nice enough face to look at every day. Ah, here comes such a man right now."

She straightened her dress and smiled prettily as first she and then Prudence were approached and asked to dance.

Emma watched them for a moment, standing rather awkwardly as she looked on at them, and then at the people around her.

"My goodness," she muttered. "I do believe I have become a wallflower."

She knew that no one was watching her, knew that no one cared about her standing alone, but when the duke swung by her again, Emma decided she'd had enough. She needed air. She needed space.

And, knowing this house as she did, she knew just where to find it.

CHAPTER 3

*A*s the last notes of the music came to a long, thrilling end, Giles bowed to Lady Maria, led her back to her mother, and then escaped the confines of the ballroom before his own mother could spot him and push another young lady into his arms. He strode out of the ballroom of the London mansion that he still couldn't quite believe belonged to him, into the library, and right through the French doors to the terrace outside. He could have used the ballroom doors to access the balcony but then, of course, someone would have seen him and he was sure that he would be followed by a young woman, prodded on by her mother to catch the unsuspecting duke for a moment alone.

Giles, however, was not the man to allow any decisions to be made for him. Not anymore.

He took a deep first breath of the cool, dark air, inviting it to fill his lungs and calm his body. It was nothing like the country air, but at least the mansion, surrounded by the length of its grounds, wasn't quite as condensed as the air in the center of the city.

He just needed a minute alone, to settle his nerves and to

remind himself that, despite his mother's wishes, he didn't have to make any decisions tonight. He could charm and dance all he wanted, and he could still finish out the evening a bachelor without any promises.

He walked to the balcony railing, closed his eyes, tilted his head back — and, after a moment, felt someone watching him. He whipped around, readying himself to turn and flee back into the library as soon as he could so as not to be caught in a compromising position — and relaxed when he saw who had joined him.

"Lady Emma," he greeted the girl who was nearly as much of a fixture around the house as his sisters themselves. Emma and Juliana had been friends since they were just children, and Giles had been somewhat shocked when he had returned a year ago to find that she had grown just as his sisters had. He supposed that's what happened, however, when one left his family for five years. He had found times to meet with his sisters, whereas Emma had been a surprise.

"Your Grace," she said with a curtsey. "I came out for some air. I had no idea you would be here. In fact—were you not just on the dance floor?"

Giles couldn't help himself. She might be his sister's best friend, but she was still a woman. He winked at her. "Watching me, were you?"

"No! I simply—"

"I'm jesting," he placated her. "Thank you for coming tonight. I'm sure Juliana was happy to have you here. It's the first time we've had people in the house — well, besides you and my mother's close friends — for such a long time."

"Of course. I will always be here for Juliana," she said, and Giles could tell that she meant it. He wondered what it would be like to have a friend so close that loyalty was never in question. He had many acquaintances — more than most men — but he wasn't sure there were many he could count on to be there for him without question.

"What do you think of it?"

"Think of what?"

"This monstrosity of an event my mother has held."

"Oh," she said, her cheeks turning pink. "It is very… grand."

"Come, Lady Emma, you were always one to say what is on your mind."

She paused for a moment, pursing her lips, and Giles was struck by how pretty she looked when she tilted her head like that, a lock of hair not quite blond, not quite brown, brushing against her cheek.

She wore a dress he knew his mother would approve of. It was not the virginal white that his sisters abhorred, but a dress that was somewhere between cream and a butter yellow — he couldn't quite tell in the light of the moon and the few sconces that were lit. It was proper for a young woman but also highlighted curves he'd never known she had. Curves that… called to him, damnit.

"The ballroom looks lovely, though I am not sure you could fit one more person in that room. I believe the entirety of the *ton* is inside at the moment."

Giles laughed, knowing she was right. "Even those who hate society are here due to morbid curiosity."

"I believe that is true," Emma said with a nod. "If it's not to see whether you will choose a woman to court tonight, then it is to try to determine how your family is faring and what happened to your father."

Giles sobered, nodding. "They think I killed him."

"I didn't say that," she said in a rush, moving closer to him, placing a gloved hand on his arm for just a minute as she looked up at him earnestly, and as he gazed into eyes that he noted were a stormy sea green, he realized one thing — he believed her. And somehow, despite not caring what anyone thought, it mattered that she believed him. Perhaps it was because this was a person who knew him, who knew his family, who was more aware than anyone without the surname Remington what he felt about this life.

"I know you didn't," he said softly. "But it is true. They all believe I killed him. It doesn't overly matter what they think, though, does it?"

"No," she said softly, snatching her hand back as if his arm had burned her. "I suppose it doesn't."

She turned from him, looking out over the grounds below.

"Your cherry trees are beautiful," she said, surprising him with the sudden change in subject. "We've struggled with ours — in the country, of course, for we do not have the room in the city. You would be one of the few who does. I suppose it could be the difference in climate. I was just thinking, in the center of the green out there, you could create a beautiful garden bed, one that could feature the grandest of flowerbeds that could be seen from the house. I've always thought a bed of rose bushes of all types would be so striking. Perhaps—"

She stopped, those lips tightening together again, before she turned to him with a small smile of self-admonishment. "I'm sorry. I was rambling."

"I had forgotten how much you enjoyed the greenery," he said, wondering why it bothered him how many times she said the word bed in one conversation. "I remember you as a girl, running off to spend time with the gardeners. There was one day, when you came with us to the country, that no one could find you for hours. Until you emerged covered from head to toe in dirt. My mother was beside herself."

Emma chuckled, a low, deep chuckle. Giles felt it vibrate through his own chest and down his body, sending strange tremors through him, which he pushed to the side as he realized that Emma was also shaking slightly.

"Are you cold?" he asked, but even as she shook her head, he slipped off his jacket and wrapped it around her shoulders.

"Here," he said. "This should help."

* * *

EMMA OPENED HER MOUTH, and then closed it again. She was surrounded by Giles Remington, Duke of Warwick. His scent, masculine and musky, like leather-bound books stacked upon shelves in a study, encompassed her, radiating from both his jacket and the man himself. She had forgotten what a *presence* he was. He seemed to take up the entirety of the terrace. She had seen him often in passing, of course, as she spent so much time with Juliana. But she wasn't sure that they had ever had a conversation just the two of them, nor had they ever been alone together.

Emma was well aware that this was not a situation in which she should remain. Yet, somehow, she couldn't seem to make herself leave.

"Thank you," she finally managed, as she *had* been cold but hadn't wanted to say anything. "Although I should be going in."

"I'm not too worried," Giles said with a wink. "You're not about to run inside saying I've compromised you and we must marry, now are you?"

Emma's mouth dropped open.

"Of course not," she said. "I would never marry you."

She snapped her jaw shut as soon as the words emerged. She hadn't meant to say them — not at all. She had simply been thinking them, and in her bid to assure him that she would never entrap him into marriage, they had come tumbling out.

She waited for him to be affronted at the insult, waited for him to take back his jacket and ask her to leave — but then he did something she would never have guessed he would.

He laughed. And he didn't just laugh politely — he threw back his head and let out a long guffaw, one that came from deep in his belly.

After a moment of shock, Emma couldn't help it — she laughed with him.

When they had both finally recovered and their laughs turned to low chuckles, Emma bit her lip and looked up at him with an apology. "I shouldn't have said that — I am so sorry," she said.

"It's absolutely fine," he returned. "It is refreshing to hear what one really thinks. Most people just tell me what I want to hear — with the exception of the women in my family, of course."

"Of course," she agreed, her lips twisting with humour once more.

"I am curious, however," he said, leaning on the wall of the balcony and staring down at her. "Why would a woman not *want* to marry a rich, young, duke?"

Emma's cheeks warmed and she found herself unable to look him in the eye, which was a rather odd sensation for her, as she was always one who faced everyone and everything head-on.

"Well," she said, trying to find the right words, "I am determined to marry for love."

Goodness, that sounded trite. And foolish. But it was the truth.

"You don't think you could find that with me?"

"I—" Emma paused, telling herself to stop and, for once,

THE MYSTERY OF THE DEBONAIR DUKE

think about what she was going to say before it came spewing out of her mouth. "I think you are a very fine man. It's just, well, I would like a husband who would stay true to me and want *only* me... if you understand. I do not mean that as an affront, Your Grace, I truly don't. Many women would have no issue with... ah... sharing if it meant being a duchess. But I do."

Her cheeks were aflame now, and Emma wished she had never started down this path of explanation. She had been trying her utmost to say what she meant without *actually* saying it, but somehow this had gone entirely wrong.

"I should really get back now," she said in a rush, deciding it would be best that she remove herself from this conversation. "I'm so sorr—"

Giles shrugged, although his expression was inscrutable as he looked out over the balcony. "I asked and you told the truth. That is more than most people would have given me."

"I know, but I never meant—"

He reached out and surprised her by catching her chin between his thumb and forefinger. "Do not be sorry. I understand what you are saying. I have certainly created a reputation for myself."

"You haven't done anything wrong," she said, shaking her head furiously. "I suppose I would simply prefer a husband who was a little less... experienced."

He laughed, but this laugh was not one of humor — it was more self-deprecating, and Emma was ashamed with her insult.

"How old are you, Lady Emma?" he asked suddenly.

"Three and twenty."

"Ah. That would be the same as Juliana, then?"

"Yes."

"And how do you know such ways of the world?"

"I believe most women know more than you think. They just don't speak of it."

"Not like you."

"I've never been able to help myself, I'm afraid."

Giles smiled. "Don't change, Lady Emma. Promise me that.'

"Very well," she agreed. "That I can do. I really should return, though. I do wish you the best in your quest. I hope you find a wife who is everything you are looking for."

"Thank you," he said softly as she shrugged out of his jacket, instantly feeling the chill with the loss of its embrace. She shivered as she passed it back to him, before turning back to make her way around the terrace to the ballroom again. She had only come this far because she wanted a better view of the grove of trees on this side. Little had she known what had been waiting for her.

Nor why their exchange had left her so shaken.

CHAPTER 4

*G*iles watched Emma walk back along the terrace, her footsteps quick, as though she had suddenly realized just how cold it was out here and was running back to the warmth and safety of the ballroom. It had been a while since a woman had amused him as she did. He wasn't lying — he did find her refreshing, even as her assessment and dismissal of him somewhat stung.

The one woman who actually knew a bit about him was the very one who didn't want him.

She did, however, have a few assumptions about him that were untrue, although it was not exactly her fault that she thought such a thing. He had been sure to cultivate quite the rakish reputation for himself. It wasn't difficult. He found it easy to charm women and he enjoyed going out to his clubs. He just wasn't quite as — how did Emma put it? — *experienced* as most people assumed. He had developed the reputation simply to spite his father.

Never before, however, had it actually bothered him to be thought of in such a way.

As he began the inevitable return to the ballroom —

taking the library route once again — Giles couldn't help but reflect on the difference between Emma and a woman like Lady Maria. He had heard his mother sigh about Juliana's choice in friends, telling his sister that while she loved Emma like a daughter, the woman was never going to find herself a husband with the way she conducted herself.

"How is the poor girl ever going to catch a man with a tongue so sharp and fingers so dirty?" she would say of Emma's propensity for gardening, a hobby that *was* rather odd for the daughter of an earl, but who was he to judge? While his mother's words would come with a warning to her own daughters, their grandmother was always quick with a word of defense for Emma, which seemed to bear more weight for her grandchildren.

Funny how Emma had grown up so suddenly and completely. Three-and-twenty, he mused, rubbing his chin as he walked through the grand archway and back into the ballroom. The domed ceiling with its painted cherubs was the inspiration for his mother's theme, and it seemed to have had its desired effect. Somehow, he had thought of Emma as much younger than that, but he supposed that a seven-year age difference had been much more evident when they were children.

"Giles!" He had barely taken one step into the room and his mother had found him. "Where have you been?"

"I'm here now," he said with a shrug. "Does that not count?"

"Well," she said, squaring her shoulders. "You've danced but a handful of times. Are there not any other women you might have an interest in? There is Lady Liliana over there. She is a lovely young lady and has a significant dowry."

"You do know that we are not in need of a significant dowry."

"It doesn't hurt, though, does it?"

Giles had to refrain from rolling his eyes, but before he could do so, he noticed another figure walking across the room — one he had seen the back of just moments before. He couldn't help that draw to her, that desire to hear more of what she had to say. At least he knew the conversation would have substance.

"Perhaps I shall dance with Lady Emma."

"Lady Emma?" One would have thought he had told his mother he was going to dance with a scandalous widow who would further ruin his reputation. "Juliana's friend?"

"Yes. Is there another Lady Emma?"

"Do not be impertinent. Why ever would you dance with her?"

"Why not?" he shrugged. "She is a young woman, and one that I know better than most others in this room."

"Yes, but what does that matter? She is most certainly not a woman you could ever entertain as your wife."

"I was going to dance with her, Mother, not marry her," he said dryly. "Besides, she's practically a child still."

"Well, I wouldn't say she is a *child* as she is the same age as Juliana, who should be married by now," his mother sniffed. "But she is not duchess material, darling. Ah, here is Lady Maria again. Perhaps one more dance?"

"I think not, Mother, that would have her believing that I—"

"Lady Maria," his mother said as the young woman approached. "You are such a lovely dancer. His Grace was just telling me that he was looking forward to dancing with you once more."

"Oh," Lady Maria said, her lips parting, seemingly shocked by the idea. "Of course, Your Grace."

Giles gritted his teeth. This would set tongues wagging now, but that wasn't what was bothering him. It was more so the expectations that would be raised within Lady Maria herself. Despite his reputation, he wasn't intent on breaking any hearts. But there was no declining this without insulting her. He held out a hand and led her onto the dance floor.

* * *

"Giles is dancing with Lady Maria again!" Juliana hissed to Emma, who had rejoined her in their place on the side of the ballroom. "I can hardly believe it. Although I suppose she is just the kind of woman who Giles needs as a duchess."

Emma didn't say anything — she couldn't, not at the moment. She was still a bit flustered from her own encounter with the duke. The man in question turned and winked at her as he passed them by, and a little flutter in her belly reminded her that it seemed they now held a secret between the two of them.

"Did Giles just look over here and wink?" Juliana asked with a frown, never one to miss anything. "What do you think that is supposed to mean?"

Emma looked around, but Prudence was nowhere to be found, so it seemed that she had no choice but to be the one to answer her friend.

"I have no idea," she said. "Perhaps he is trying to tell you something?"

"It's rather peculiar," Juliana mused, "but it almost seemed as though he were looking at you."

Emma snorted. "That's ridiculous. It was probably both of us together, as I am sure that I am nearly as much of a sister to him as you are."

"That's true," Juliana said with a warm smile. "You are practically family by now."

Emma's smile this time was a true one, for she did value Juliana's friendship more than nearly anything else in her life.

"It is odd, isn't it, that whoever he marries will be like a new sister to you? Living with you, taking charge of the household?"

"That should be interesting with Mother around," Juliana said with a laugh. "I suppose she might have to eventually find somewhere else to live, although I cannot see her going quietly."

Emma tried to imagine living with the woman who would become the dowager duchess watching over her shoulder. She couldn't help but shudder. The duchess had always accepted her in the house, but she hadn't hidden the fact that she didn't entirely approve of Emma and had suggested through veiled comments that perhaps Emma should change her ways if she wished to find a husband. She was right, of course, but Emma didn't want a husband who wouldn't accept her for who she was. She knew that was ridiculous, but it was the truth.

"Where is your mother tonight?" Juliana asked.

"Feeling poorly again, as always," Emma murmured. Her mother was always feeling poorly, although Emma had come to understand that her mother had an aversion to social situations more than she was actually unwell. Her father didn't seem to overly care, as it allowed him to accompany Emma and stay in the card room for the entirety of the evening without having to worry over his wife. Emma had spent her life with somewhat distracted parents, not having any siblings herself. She had been born after years of despair that her parents would never have a child, and she could only imagine how disappointed her father had been when she was born a girl.

Nevertheless, he had never actually allowed her to feel that way. He was just… distant.

"Where did you go?" Juliana asked now.

"When?" Emma said, trying to feign nonchalance. She had

a feeling that if she told Juliana she had been talking to her brother on the terrace that Juliana would make much more out of it than it actually was.

"When I was dancing."

"I was here," Emma said. "You must not have seen me."

"That's funny. I could have sworn I saw you going out on the terrace."

They both turned at the new voice that had joined their conversation, and Emma didn't hold back her grimace when she saw who it was. Lady Christina Dennison, a woman who she would be happy to never have to see again in her life. She was the worst type — the one who saw every other woman as her competition.

"Did you have a little tryst, Lady Emma?"

"Of course not," Emma said with a snort as she turned her head away.

"Or perhaps you just went out to dirty your hands in the gardens."

Emma did not turn to respond. The truth was, Lady Christina was partially right, but she wasn't going to give her the satisfaction of knowing it.

"Well, at least we know you weren't with the duke," Christina said with a little trill of laughter, and if it wouldn't have ruined both her own reputation as well as Giles', Emma would have gladly told Christina just how wrong she was.

"Not that it matters," Juliana said hotly in defense of her friend, "but why would that not be?"

"He would never be interested in a woman like Emma," Christina said with a snort as she adjusted her already-perfect white lace gloves. "You know you are a disaster, Emma, a fact which His Grace likely already knows. You could hardly look after a house — or its master — from the gardens."

"Now see here," Juliana said, her hands in a fist at her

hips, the other lifted to shake in Christina's face, her temper getting the better of her.

As much as Emma appreciated it and would have liked to have told Christina herself just what she thought of her accusations, she had no wish to see Juliana find herself in any sort of trouble due to coming to her defense.

"It's fine, Juliana," she said, placing a hand on her friend's, lowering the finger Juliana had set in Lady Christina's face. "Some things are not worth the trouble."

With a pointed look at Lady Christina before the woman flounced away, Emma and Juliana paused for a moment before they both burst out laughing.

"She's just jealous," Juliana said.

"Of what?"

"Of the fact that you have even spoken to my brother," Juliana said. "At least he is smart enough to never go for a viper like her. Not to worry, I was sure to tell him which women were best to avoid."

"That's good of you," Emma commented.

"It is actually self-serving, as you are right. I will have to spend the rest of my life with the woman he marries in the family," Juliana admitted.

Emma could only chuckle at her friend before she sobered slightly. For while she didn't entirely believe in Christina's words, tonight had made one thing clear. She was not the woman for a man like Giles, Duke of Warwick. And he was not the man for her. She needed a husband who would allow her to continue to do what she loved to do, while being patient and kind and understanding and loving. Was that too much to ask?

As Giles danced by again, his eyes on her as they passed, she wondered why all her requirements didn't seem quite as important as they had been before tonight.

CHAPTER 5

*E*mma checked the large clock that hung in the entrance hall one more time.

Half-past three now. Juliana was supposed to have arrived at least thirty minutes ago. While Juliana wasn't always perfectly punctual, it wasn't like her to be *this* late. She would normally have sent a note if she had been so held up.

Not that they had anywhere important to go. They were simply going to walk to the circulating library. But Emma had left Bernard and the small garden plot behind her family's townhouse early in order to clean up. Juliana would have understood not to waste her time.

"Lydia!" she said to her maid, who was patiently waiting by the entrance of the front foyer that opened up into the drawing room, "I believe we shall have to go find Juliana ourselves. Hopefully, we don't cross paths on the way over."

Fortunately, they didn't live very far away — Emma's family's townhouse was just off Berkeley Square, while Warwick House was a few streets east. Emma cut across the square, although she kept her eyes searching the perimeter in case she spotted Juliana.

As she walked through the front gates and then up the grand staircase of the mansion Juliana called home, Emma couldn't help but wonder whether the duke might be in today. She supposed if he was, he would be ensconced in his study or his library. What he did all day in there, she had no idea. It was hard to picture the Giles she had known as a youth enjoying poring over ledgers or meeting men of business. She could not think of a less serious, studious type of man than the current Duke of Warwick.

The smile was still on her face when she knocked on the front door and the butler allowed her entrance, although he wore a rather confused smile of welcome.

"Lady Emma," Jameson said with a nod as he led her inside. "Is Lady Juliana not with you?"

"No," she said, shaking her head. "She was supposed to meet me at my home but when she didn't arrive, I thought I would see what had kept her."

"I shall find the duchess," he said. "One moment."

"Emma?" It was Prudence who first joined her in the front parlor. It was not the most formal room of the house but one of the most comfortable. A red, blue, and cream rug had been laid over blond hardwood, while floral curtains surrounded each window. Emma ignored any of the chairs situated strategically throughout the room. "Juliana left to your house over an hour ago."

"How odd," Emma said, scratching her nose. "She never arrived."

The air in the room seemed to shift, and Emma knew before even looking up who had entered.

"What is the problem?"

He looked delightfully ruffled, his cravat slightly askew and his hair standing straight up as though he had been running his hand through it, likely in frustration over the very books Emma had pictured him bent over.

"Juliana was to meet Emma at her home but never arrived."

Giles' normally jovial face narrowed in concern. "How long ago was this?"

"An hour ago," Emma responded. "When she didn't arrive, I thought I would come see for myself what had kept her."

"That's not like her," Giles said, his eyes on Emma as though she held all the answers he was searching for. "Is it? No. Was there anywhere — or anyone — she might otherwise meet?"

Emma knew exactly what he was asking but immediately shook her head.

"No. Not Juliana. If there was anyone, I would know."

Giles took a deep breath. "Very well. Perhaps she got distracted and you missed her on the way. I shall walk you back."

She could tell he was agitated but trying not to show it and she had the strange urge to go over to him and tell him that all was going to be fine.

She opened her mouth to say something of the sort, but as she did the front door burst open and Jameson grimaced in horror as Juliana's maid banged the door open and stumbled through, breathing heavily, her bonnet askew.

"Abigail!" Jameson said in admonishment. "What in the heavens—"

"It's fine, Jameson," Giles said, stretching his hand out to urge the man to cease. "Abigail, where is Juliana?"

When Abigail looked up, tears stained her cheeks and she was panting so hard that Emma wasn't sure if she was ever going to say anything. "She—that is—I tried—I—oh, I am so sorry!"

She collapsed in a torrent of tears, and Emma rushed over and placed an arm around the girl's shoulders before leading her over to one of the pink-striped sofas. "Perhaps we can have some water?" she asked another maid who had come rushing to the door of the room along with a few of the staff, word of the commotion upstairs having drawn a crowd.

"Or brandy," Giles muttered as one of the maids scurried away, and Abigail finally took a deep, shuddery breath before she lifted her eyes to them.

"We were walking down the street, and she was right next to me," she said, although her words took a lot longer than any of them would have liked, for they were broken up by the hiccups of her sobs. "There was a commotion in front of one of the houses — something to do with a horse, I'm not entirely sure — and I paused to watch. When I turned back around… Lady Juliana was gone."

"Gone?" Giles repeated, incredulity in his tone. "What do you mean, gone?"

"I-I mean, she just wasn't there. It was as though she had entirely disappeared, or that she had never been there to begin with."

"Where was this?" Emma asked, her chest full of panic even as she tried to keep her words soft so as to keep the girl calm.

"At the other end of the square," the girl said, pointing out the window. "There were not that many people about and it was only just a moment, I swear."

"It wasn't your fault," Emma said, patting her hand, finding that comforting the maid was distracting her from her own panic. She looked up to Giles, surprised at how calm he remained. "It doesn't make sense, though. Juliana had promised she was going to meet me. If she was trying to go somewhere alone — which she wouldn't have without telling me or Prudence, I just know it — she would never have made that commitment."

Giles took a visible breath before running a hand once more through his already well-mussed hair as he paced two steps forward and backward in front of the entrance. He opened his mouth, but before he could say anything, his mother came flying into the room, in a state of half-dress.

"Will someone please tell me what is going on? I was trying to call for a cup of tea and it seemed the entirety of the house had absconded to this parlor, although why I—"

It seemed she had finally taken a moment to look at Giles, for her face drained of color. "What is it? Is something amiss?"

"It's Juliana," he said, the words coming out nearly gutted. "She's disappeared."

* * *

THERE WAS a moment of shocked silence around the room before it seemed like all erupted in one moment.

"Disappeared!" his mother nearly shrieked. "Whatever do you mean?"

Giles explained the situation as best and as hurriedly as he could, but he didn't have much time to make sure she stayed calm. Juliana was his responsibility, and he had to find her, especially to make sure that nothing happened to her.

"Where could she have gone?" He looked around the room at all of them, his eyes finally settling on Emma. She would know better than any of them what Juliana might have been thinking, although even she seemed perplexed by this entire situation.

Emma stood, wringing her hands together.

"Anywhere I can think of we would have gone together. Unless…" a pained expression crossed her face, "unless she decided she preferred going alone? Although I'm sure she would have told me."

His mother stepped up from behind him. "Perhaps she

felt that certain influences were not helping her marriage prospects."

"That's enough, Mother," Giles snapped. He didn't need his mother's veiled pettiness in this situation, even as he realized that she was as worried as the rest of them were and allowing her emotions to get the better of her. "Right now, we only need helpful suggestions. I'm going to go out and look for Juliana. Mother, you stay here in case she returns home."

His mother also would be no help roaming the streets.

"Pru, you better stay with Mother," he decided, even as his sister opened her mouth to protest before he finished his sentence. "Grandmother is likely upstairs in her room. Don't bother her."

"It's too late for that," came a voice from the hallway, and he closed his eyes and took another breath, although he knew that his grandmother would likely have as good an idea as anyone on what to do. "Where could the girl have gone?"

Giles tamped down the dread as he was reminded that his family had gone through another loss in the not-so-distant past. But his father's death and Juliana's disappearance could have nothing to do with one another — could they?

No, his sister was a twenty-three-year-old woman likely after a little independence. They would start there and not let themselves wonder anything further.

"Lady Emma, you accompanied her most often," he said, turning to her, strangely finding some comfort in her presence and her practical approach to most matters. "Can you make a list of places where she might have gone? Jameson, will you have one of the boys saddle my horse?"

"I'm coming with you."

They all turned to see Emma still standing, arms rigid by her side, hands fisted in determination.

"You are what?"

"I'm coming with you," she repeated. "It's like you said. I know Juliana better than anyone. I know what she would be thinking. Making a list isn't enough as you might miss something."

"She is my sister," he argued. "I—"

"Giles." Prudence walked across the room and gently placed a hand on his arm. "Emma is right. You do know Jules, but you don't know her like Emma does."

He swallowed, knowing she was right, although it was a harsh reminder of the guilt that plagued him. For when he left his father behind, he had left the rest of his family as well, and he wasn't sure his relationship with his sisters would ever fully recover.

"Very well," he said nodding at her. "We go shortly. We'll take the phaeton. It will be the fastest way for the two of us to search."

Emma nodded, resolve replacing the distress in her eyes, which he was happy about. A panicked woman wasn't going to be any help to him, although Emma had never struck him as the type of woman to allow her emotions to get the better of her.

The woman might have been averse to marrying a man like him, but he hoped she could bring herself to follow his direction for enough time it took to locate Juliana.

He bid farewell to the rest of his family as he hurried her toward the front entrance, where the stable hands had worked quickly to prepare their ride.

"Well?" he said as they walked outside into sunshine that seemed far too bright for such stormy circumstances. "Where to first, my expert on all things Juliana?"

CHAPTER 6

*E*mma didn't appreciate his mocking tone.

"You do know I am as worried as you are, and that I am here to help you, do you not?" she asked, even as she took his offered hand to help her up into the phaeton. She had never ridden in one before.

She'd had gentleman callers, of course, but for the most part, they had sat stiffly in her mother's sitting room as her mother sat on one corner of the sofa without saying anything and Emma awkwardly said all the wrong things. She was a bit straightforward most of the time anyway, but when she felt uncomfortable, it was another situation entirely.

One had taken her for a couple of rides along Rotten Row in his carriage before asking for her hand, but she had been so bored on those hour-long excursions that she could hardly imagine a lifetime with the man.

She had felt rather guilty about that one, though. He had been so crestfallen.

She had been much relieved when she later found out

that he was primarily after her dowry and not affected one way or another by her character.

"I am sorry," Giles muttered now. "I do appreciate your help. I just cannot understand why Juliana would do such a thing."

He flicked the reins and sent the horses into motion, startling Emma, who fell against his side before pushing herself back upright. Spring had arrived and she found herself instantly warming, likely from the temperature and her worry for Juliana. She tugged at the neck of her cloak which suddenly seemed too tight.

"I suppose we should try the bookstore first," Emma said, pointing him down Piccadilly. Giles nodded before Emma continued, answering his previous question. "I honestly have no idea why she would have had such a wish to go anywhere alone. But we'll find her."

She stole a glance over at Giles as her left hand clutched the rail of the phaeton in order to keep her seat. His normally relaxed jaw was tight, his eyes narrowed, his cheek twitchy, and she couldn't help herself from lifting her right hand and placing it on top of his fists, which were clenching the reins in an unyielding grip.

He looked over at her in surprise, his nostrils slightly flaring, and she managed a weak smile, tamping down her own worry as she tried to comfort him.

The bookstore was close, but the concerned Mrs. Hondros who worked at the desk shook her head and told Emma that she hadn't seen Juliana since the last time the two of them had visited. She promised to ask around and see if she could determine whether or not anyone had seen her, but before Emma could properly thank her, Giles had placed a hand on the small of her back and was propelling her back out the door and to the phaeton.

"We cannot be rude!" she protested, but he was shaking his head.

"We can apologize later," he said, wrapping his large hands around her waist and lifting her into the phaeton as if she weighed nothing. Emma opened her mouth to protest, but he was already around the other side, jumping up and putting them into motion. This time, at least, she knew to hold on tightly as they started forward.

"The museum," she gasped as she brought one hand to her head to make sure that her bonnet was firmly in place, the other back on the rail as they went flying.

He nodded grimly and they rocketed down Great Russell Street, Giles deftly avoiding the people and animals who stared up at him in shock.

"We won't be able to find Juliana if we kill ourselves — or anyone else," Emma remarked as they came to a stop in front of the British Museum's front steps. Giles' horses were a beautiful pair of chestnuts, hardly breathing heavily despite the sprint down the cobblestones.

"I am a better driver than most," he remarked matter-of-factly before they started up the stairs. They were greeted by the porter, Emma stepping in front of Giles before he took his annoyance out on the man. The museum had been robbed not long ago, and she understood why they might be affronted by a couple who looked as though they had just taken part in a race at Newbury.

"It is of a most urgent matter," Emma said. "We are looking for His Grace's sister, and she—"

"Oh, Your Grace?" the man said, his cheeks instantly reddening. "My apologies. I had no idea. I—"

"It doesn't matter," Giles cut him off, and Emma looked at him with wide eyes. In most of the time she had been acquainted with Giles, he had been the affable, charming gentleman.

There had been moments when he had been quite displeased with his father, of course, but he always seemed to avoid those situations. This Giles was not one she had ever known before, although she supposed it was the first time he was actually facing something as opposed to running away. "Have you seen my sister? Lady Juliana? Dark hair, and uh…"

He seemed at a loss as to how else to describe her.

"What was she wearing?" Emma asked Giles and he shook his head, his eyes wide and desperate.

"I have no idea."

"She would have been alone," Emma told the man. "Perhaps she would have arrived an hour ago?"

"We only opened thirty minutes ago," the porter said apologetically, but kept stealing concerned glances at Giles as though he was waiting for him to take a swing at him. "I haven't seen her."

Emma nodded and thanked the man before she followed Giles back down the magnificent staircase.

"Did you know that it had just opened?"

"I did, but I forgot," she said, and could practically feel Giles' anger radiating off him, which annoyed her, as she knew it was misplaced, and she had only made a mistake in her own concern.

"Where to now?" he asked, and Emma nibbled her lip, for the truth was, she truly had no idea. They could continue to run around London all day and never get anywhere. "Where would she go that she wouldn't want you to go along with her?"

Emma thought on that. There was one place. But to tell Giles would be to confess one of Juliana's secrets, one that Emma didn't quite feel at liberty to share.

A quick glance up at Giles, though, and she knew that she didn't have much of a choice.

"There is one possibility," she said slowly.

"Which is?"

"It's not somewhere that is usually active during the day, however," she said, taking his hand as he helped her up this time instead of hoisting her up.

"Emma, you had better tell me what you are talking about without speaking in riddles, and you had better tell me very quickly."

Had the situation not been so dire, Emma would have rolled her eyes right in Giles' face.

"Very well. Did you know that Juliana does not eat any meat?"

"Yes. It was of great consternation to my father."

"Well, we were at a lecture a while ago and Juliana began speaking with another young woman, and as it turned out, they had this particular preference in common. Then the young woman told her—"

"Emma, please get to the heart of the matter."

"Yes, right. It is a society of like-minded people who have the interests of animals at heart and who prefer not to eat them."

"Of all the—"

Emma held up a hand. "It is not for us to judge. They actually have some valid points."

Giles sat with his hands on the reins. "Where are they, Emma?"

"They meet at the home of one of the founding members."

Giles gritted his teeth. "Who is?"

"Mrs. Adelaide Stone. She lives in Holborn. Close to Lincoln's Inn Fields."

"Well, Mrs. Adelaide Stone has some explaining to do."

As she stood next to Giles on the steps of a small but tidy house a short time later, Emma couldn't shake the feeling that this was all wrong. She had met Mrs. Stone before and she was a lovely woman, who had five children and a husband who worked hard. She could hardly imagine that Juliana would have escaped for a day at her home. They usually met in the evenings, when Juliana would sneak out, long after Giles had left for his clubs or other such pursuits.

And every time, Juliana told Emma where she was going, so that if any questions arose, Emma could say that Juliana had been with her.

Mrs. Stone answered the door herself with a warm if somewhat harried smile. "May I help you?"

"We are looking for Lady Juliana," Emma said before Giles could get a word in edgewise. Normally she would be pleased to have Giles do the talking for he could charm a mouse out of its hole, but today he was a different man. "Would she happen to be here today?"

"Lady Juliana? No, not today," Mrs. Stone said, shaking her head in confusion. "I haven't seen her since our meeting last week."

Giles' eye twitched again, but Emma thought it best that she refrain from commenting upon it.

"If you see her, will you please tell her to return home immediately?" Giles said through tight teeth.

"Of course," said Mrs. Stone before her eyes widened. "Oh, Your Grace, forgive me." She sank into a curtsey despite the toddler on her hip. "My apologies. I had no idea."

"I can see that," he said. "My sister will not be coming to your meetings any longer."

"I am sorry to hear that," Mrs. Stone said, lifting her eyes to him. She had obviously been showing deference to the duke because of his station, but she also did not seem to be a woman who would back down easily. "I do think she found herself quite at home here, however, so I hope that you will reconsider once you have a chance to talk to her."

"I will be talking to her about it, that is for certain," Giles said tersely. "We must continue on."

"Wait!" Mrs. Stone said as Giles started down the stairs. "Is she missing?"

"She is," Emma said, despite Giles' impatient look. "But hopefully not for long."

She turned around one more time and whispered to Mrs. Stone, "we will get this sorted, not to worry."

They sat in the phaeton, then, in front of Mrs. Stone's small red brick townhouse, the silence stretching ominously between them.

"Well?" Giles said, staring straight ahead of him. "What now?"

"I think all we can do now is return home and see if perhaps Juliana has returned," Emma said dejectedly. "I'm not sure where else to go."

Giles shocked her then by leaning forward and placing his head in his hands.

"I just don't know what to do," he said, his voice muffled. "I am supposed to be the one looking after my sisters, my family, and I have already failed them. I suppose it's nothing new."

"You have done nothing of the sort," Emma said, heat in her words as she realized that she meant it. She had resented Giles, as Juliana had, for abandoning them, but she had also witnessed enough to know that he had reasons for doing so. "You are out here, searching for your sister, when others would have just waited for her to return. I believe the fact that you care says more than anything else ever could."

He raised his head from his hands, turning it to meet her eyes. "I just wish more than anything when we return home that she is there waiting for us."

"I hope so too," Emma said fervently.

"Thank you," he said, and Emma forced a smile to her face to try to comfort him.

"Of course," she said.

45

While Emma would never have wished for the circumstances that caused it, this vulnerability she had seen within him today was both shocking and concerting. Somehow it seemed much easier to know that he was a consistent, charming, rakish presence. Perhaps not a man who one could rely on to always be there, but one that could always be relied on to be the man she had expected him to be.

Today he had shown another side of himself — and the surliness, the rudeness? She was not sure that it was a side she liked. He had been unpredictable. And if there was one thing Emma appreciated, it was the predictable reliability of all in her life.

Giles had just proven that he was anything but.

CHAPTER 7

There had been a few truly terrible days in Giles life — most notably the one when he had shut the door of Warwick House in his father's face and hadn't returned — but this one topped them all.

At least he hadn't been alone today, he thought as he started up the stairs to the front door. When he had helped Emma out of the phaeton, he hadn't been able to resist his need to have her — her or anyone, he wasn't sure — close to him, and he'd held out his arms on the pretense of assisting her down. When she had then slipped her fingers around his elbow, he had hugged her hand against his body, scaring himself with his need for their attachment.

They were connected, by their concern for Juliana if nothing else, and he knew that he owed Emma an apology for his surliness today. But that could come later. For right now, he had to go in and determine the next steps to finding Juliana.

Jameson opened the door before Giles reached for the knob, and he instantly knew from the butler's countenance that Juliana hadn't yet returned.

"There's something else, isn't there?" Giles stated, and Jameson nodded.

"A note that just came. I haven't even had a chance to take it to your mother yet as you nearly followed right behind the boy."

Giles held out his hand and Jameson placed the folded paper within. Giles ripped the seal and immediately read the message, his heart hammering so hard in his chest he thought it might explode right out of it as he realized what the words meant. He dropped his arm to his side, and Emma plucked it out of his fingers. He heard her gasp in shock as she brought a hand to cover her mouth, and then she was tugging on his sleeve, breaking him out of his stupor.

"Giles, she's... she's—"

"Yes." He stared at the paper held between Emma's delicate fingers, seemingly so innocent and yet holding such malice.

"What do we do?"

"*I* go."

"But—"

Emma was interrupted, however, when his mother, sister, and a few moments later, his grandmother, appeared in the doorway.

"Did you find her?" his mother asked, but Prudence was already shaking her head.

"What's wrong? What is it?" she asked, apparently accurately reading their expressions.

Giles opened his mouth but found the words wouldn't quite form. He tried twice, until finally Emma spoke for them both, choking the words out.

"A note arrived. It seems that Juliana... has been taken."

There was a moment of stunned silence before all three women began speaking at the same time, and, not for the first time in his life, Giles wished that he had brothers. An older brother would have been much preferable, for then he could have dealt with this situation and any others that might have arisen.

"What do you mean, she has been taken?" Prudence demanded.

"A note arrived," Giles finally said. "It is addressed to me. If I would like to see Juliana again, I am to go to this address tonight just after sundown."

"And do what? For what reason?" his mother demanded, but Giles just lifted his hands in helpless supplication.

"I have no idea. But I have to go."

His family began talking again, and it wasn't until they finally stopped that he realized Emma hadn't said a word since the lot of them had arrived.

"You cannot go." Her words were so quiet that he almost didn't hear them.

"Pardon me?"

"You cannot go," she said, louder this time, her stormy blue-green eyes rising to meet his, and for a moment he had a crazy notion to forget everything else and drown himself in them. "It's a trap. It has to be. Why go through all of this trouble only to give her back to you?"

"Of course it is a trap," he said impatiently, "but what else am I supposed to do? If I don't go, we might never see her again."

His mother let out a whimper, but to her credit, she was still standing strongly on her own feet.

"This is ridiculous," she said. "We must go to Bow Street. Surely, they can help."

"They could," Emma agreed, "but the note specifically says not to. Perhaps the kidnappers can somehow track the activities of the detectives. Or perhaps they would be too conspicuous."

"She's right," Giles said, although it rather pained him to say it. "I must go alone."

"You cannot," Emma repeated. "It would be stupidity."

He whirled around on her, his frustration at the entire situation catching up with him. "How can you say that? I thought you loved my sister!"

"I do!" she said, her eyes going from sad and pitiful to blazing at him in an instant. "How could you ever suggest that I don't?"

"By the very fact that you do not want me to go after her. What kind of friend is that?"

"A friend," she said, lifting a finger and surprising him by poking him — hard — in the chest, "who does not want her very best friend, a woman who is like a sister to her, to spend the rest of her life awash in guilt because her abduction led to her brother's murder. A friend who wants to make sure that her best friend can come home to the family that she left. A friend who has been by your side all late afternoon, trying to find her!"

As she had spoken her heated words, she had stepped closer to him, until now they were standing but inches apart, her head tilted back to look up into his face, and for a moment — one unprecedented, uncontrollable moment — Giles had the strangest sensation to lean down, take her face between his hands, and kiss the hell out of her. To let all that they had been feeling course through them and into one another, to take and give and find some kind of relief.

He nearly did so.

Until Prudence cleared her throat and stepped toward them, and Emma jumped back hastily. Giles ran a hand through his hair. He had completely forgotten that they had an audience.

"This foyer is too small for all of us," he muttered, shocked at what he had nearly done. What had gotten into him? He hated that he had relied on Emma so heavily today. She was not only a woman, but a woman seven years his junior, his little sister's friend. One that he could remember when she had been in the nursery. She should be nothing more to him than a nuisance.

"Have food prepared, Mother. This is going to be a long day."

He looked at Emma, who stood, uncertain, in the foyer. Giles sighed. "You might as well stay," he said.

"With such a warm invitation, how could I refuse?" she said, raising an eyebrow, but she had only just crossed into the next room when there was another knock at the door. Emma turned, waiting, hope and expectation in her eyes, and Giles crossed and threw open the door himself before Jameson could do so.

But it wasn't Juliana on the other side. It was a man, one with whom Giles did have an appointment, an appointment that he had entirely forgotten.

"Your Grace!" the man said, obviously surprised that the duke himself had answered the door. He recovered quite quickly, however. "Is something amiss?"

"Yes," Giles said grimly. "And this is actually perfect timing — for I believe you can help."

EMMA HAD FELT flushed since that heated exchange in the foyer, one that she knew she had been a fool to involve herself in, but she had been so annoyed that Giles would accuse her of not wanting what was best for Juliana when all she wanted to do was protect them all.

For a moment, she had actually thought that he was going to kiss her — which must have been the events of the day catching up to her. She was a fool to imagine such a thing. It was simply that they were both passionate about seeing Juliana safe again. Thank goodness his family had been there, or she might have stood on her tiptoes and done something very, very stupid.

Now, she sat beside his mother and sister in the drawing room, staring down at her untouched tea as they waited for Giles to finish his meeting.

"Who did he say this man was?"

"A detective, Mother," Prudence answered, as calm as she always was, no matter the circumstance.

"Why does he think *this* detective can help, when he wants nothing to do with Bow Street?"

"This man is more private," Prudence said. "And Giles had already hired him."

"For what?"

"To look into Father's death."

"Whatever for?" the duchess said, fanning herself. "Why would he want to sully the family's name? I can hardly imagine—"

"Perhaps it was to protect the family," Emma said, knowing she was committing a sin by interrupting the duchess, but she could hardly sit and listen to the woman continue to rail against her family when Giles was only trying to do his best for them. "Have none of you stopped to think that perhaps there is something tying the two situations together?"

The duchess' teacup clattered loudly as she placed it back on the saucer. "Excuse me?"

Before Emma could answer, however, the duke stood in the doorway, staring down at them. "Lady Emma, will you join us, please?" he asked, his voice strained, and Emma nodded, curious but not saying anything — not at this time.

Giles ignored his mother's questions and protests as he led Emma along the corridor and into his study, where she found the new arrival sitting in one of the despicable over-stuffed mustard yellow chairs.

"Lady Emma, this is Matthew Archibald," he said, as the sandy-haired man stood and bowed to her.

"I wish we were meeting under different circumstances, Mr. Archibald," she said, and he smiled grimly.

"That is what most people say when they meet me, I'm afraid."

"I can imagine," she murmured.

Giles pointed her into the other chair while he sat in the atrocity of an iron-welded chair behind the desk. "Mr. Archibald here has been looking into my father's death."

"I wouldn't say I have been looking as of yet," Mr. Archibald amended. "I was not aware whether or not you were actually interested in discovering the truth."

"I will admit that I don't overly care about what happened to my father," Giles said, looking from Mr. Archibald to Emma and then back again. "But if it makes a difference to my family's future, then I would like to know. At least they could put the rumors to bed. But that will have to wait until we determine what has happened to Juliana. We need her back home. Lady Emma, Mr. Archibald has some questions that I… couldn't answer."

"Of course. I'm happy to try," she said. Giles eyed her with an expression that she couldn't quite place, but it looked an awful lot like he was vexed with her — although what she had done now, she had no idea.

She turned away from the bear behind the desk toward the much more approachable Mr. Archibald, although now that she had the opportunity to scrutinize him more closely, she could see that there was hardness behind his eyes, as though he had seen some sides of life that she would forever be protected from simply by her birth.

"His Grace has told me quite a bit about his sister but

suggested that perhaps you might know more. Is there anyone who might be cross with her? Anyone she has offended? Any particular controversies that she might be a part of?"

Emma shook her head throughout all of it.

"No. Juliana is one of the most cheerful women I know, and she certainly would never cause a scene."

"What about this... society she was secretly taking part in?"

"The animal protection society?" Emma wrinkled her nose. "They are a peaceful group and mean no harm. They meet because they have a common interest that not many others share."

"Humor me," Mr. Archibald said, and Emma nodded slowly. She still felt that she was sharing too much of Juliana's secret, but if it would help them find her, then so be it.

"They are concerned about the betterment of the treatment of animals. They don't eat meat and feel that there should be more humane practices to protect animals. They are on the lookout for strays and abused animals. But, thus far, they have been very quiet about their gatherings and don't share their views with anyone outside of their closest circles."

Giles snorted, and Emma looked over at him, realizing that he was hurt at being placed outside of Juliana's life.

"She was going to tell you, but she believed you would think her foolish," she said, and Giles shrugged as though it didn't mean anything. It likely normally wouldn't have, but in the current circumstances she had a feeling that it held much more weight to know he had been left out of a part of her life.

The truth was, as much as Juliana and Prudence loved their brother, he hadn't been around for a significant portion of their lives. They had met up with him now and again, but it wasn't the same as growing up with their brother in the house.

After school, he had gone to live in his own bachelor quarters. Emma couldn't help but wonder what they had been like — how the man himself had made his own way in the world.

"I really don't think this would have anything to do with her disappearance," Emma couldn't help but add, leaning forward toward the detective, who was writing notes on a pad in his lap. "Have you considered that this might be tied to the previous duke's death?"

Giles cleared his throat, and Emma knew what he was saying without words — that it wasn't her place to question the detective, nor Giles. That this was a family affair and she should stay out of it.

Well, they had brought her in this far, so now they were going to suffer the consequences of her involvement.

"I do not mean to be impertinent," she continued, "but I ask because it has not yet been mentioned, and I think it might be important in determining where Juliana has gone." She shifted her gaze from one man to the other, and Archibald looked over at Giles as though requesting permission before he spoke.

"We have not reached far enough into our investigation of the duke's death, for we were waiting for more… information before continuing," he said. "However, if the duke was, in fact, murdered, as it appears he was from what we know —" that was certainly news to Emma, news most interesting — "then it stands to reason that someone could have malice against the family."

"Perhaps, then, the question is not who Juliana might have angered," Emma said, turning toward Giles, placing her hands on the desk between them, "but who *you* have."

Giles raised one eyebrow as he looked at her as though asking if she was really going to so question him, and Emma was struck by the fact that, as much as she had felt like part of his family, this man was a powerful duke now, and who was she, a friend of his little sister, to be questioning?

But now was not the time to worry about apologies. Not while Juliana was still in danger.

"I can assure you," Giles said, leaning forward toward her, and Emma refused not to back away, "that the only person who didn't enjoy my company has now passed from this world."

"Your father," she said.

"Yes, my father," he confirmed.

"Were there any men who might be angry because of your seduction of any particular women?" she asked, keeping her voice light, although she couldn't help that ache in her breast that told her his answer mattered more to her than she would have liked.

"No," Giles said tersely and succinctly. "There are not."

"Lady Emma."

Emma had nearly forgotten the detective as he had sat quietly in the corner and witnessed their exchange. "Yes?"

"Why do you not leave the questioning to me? Though I thank you for your help."

"I fear it wasn't much help at all," Emma said, biting her lip as she felt properly chastised. "What shall we do now?"

Archibald looked toward Giles. "Leave this with me. My men and I will try to discreetly scout the area. I promise you that no one will have any idea that you hired us, if they even see us at all. Tonight, I could go in your place."

Giles was already shaking his head. "Too risky. They likely know what I look like, if they knew Juliana well enough to take her."

"Very well. If you choose to go—"

"I do."

"Then we will be there, although we will maintain a distance so that they do not know we are with you. As we cannot be close to you, you will still most certainly be putting yourself in danger. You know that?"

"Yes. And I have no issue with it."

"Very well," Mr. Archibald said, unfolding himself from the chair and nodding to Emma before bowing to Giles. "Good day, Your Grace, Lady Emma. I will report in tonight an hour before the meeting time."

"Thank you," Giles said, and when Mr. Archibald left, Emma knew that she should follow him out. But she couldn't stop staring at Giles, who was back sitting in his chair, his gaze fixed somewhere ahead of him at a point in the wall. Emma was well aware that he was staring at nothing in particular, and she could only imagine what he was seeing in his mind.

She stood, taking a step toward the door, but then paused before turning around, as she didn't seem to be able to physically move forward until she did all she could.

She walked over to the desk and crouched down next to his chair, placing one hand on the chair's hideous bronzed arm, the other on Giles' hand. Neither of them wore gloves, and his hand burned beneath hers.

"If there was ever a woman who could defend herself, it is Juliana," she said, her voice just above a whisper. "I am as worried as you are, but I *know* she will be fine. There is no way she cannot be." She squeezed his hand. "I promise you that I will do anything I can to help find her."

Finally, he turned his head, tilting it down to look at her.

"Thank you," he said, placing his other hand on top of hers, sandwiching her hand between his.

Leaving Emma to wonder just what she was supposed to do about that jump in her heart.

CHAPTER 8

*G*iles continued to stare at the door long after Emma had departed.

How could he possibly be comforted by the woman he had, for the first thirty years of his life, merged with his little sisters, while at the same time wonder about her, wanting to know more, learn more — learn about *her*? When had she developed such lush curves? When had she mastered walking with that enticing sway of her hips? And when had he all of a sudden started noticing?

The latter was one question he could actually answer. It was after their conversation at the ball his mother had held. But what did it say about him that his sister was missing — kidnapped — and he was in his study lusting after her best friend?

He ran a hand through his hair and then dropped his head into his hands. He felt so helpless. He had always known that he was failing his little sisters in some way, but never more than this moment. All he could do now was pray that Archibald would find something, and that when they went to this meeting tonight, Juliana would be there waiting, unharmed.

Until that time… he supposed he'd better check on his mother.

He had just opened the door and stepped into the hall when a familiar tapping on the floor had him turning around to greet his grandmother.

"You're in a pickle, aren't you, son?" she said as she neared. Giles nodded at her, squaring his shoulders in what he hoped was a look of strength as the head of this family. When his grandmother reached him, however, her wise eyes, as blue as his own but with many more laugh lines, staring up at him, he realized that it didn't matter how hard he tried — the title of head of this family belonged to someone else entirely. She placed a hand on his arm, squeezing just tight enough to impart some of her strength.

"I understand you feel powerless. But Juliana is a smart girl, and a strong one. If anyone can hold her own through this, it is she."

Giles nodded, swallowing the emotion that clogged his throat, as his grandmother's words reminded him of another's. Everyone had so much faith in his sister. He could only hope that they would have the same amount of faith in him when he went to find her.

* * *

ARCHIBALD ARRIVED that evening an hour before they were to depart for the meeting.

Unfortunately, he had nothing of note to impart to Giles after he was shown into the study, away from the ears of the women in the household.

"We scoured the area as best we could. It's a house on the

edge of Greenford, just outside of London. It will not take long to get there once we're outside the city with a horse or carriage. The place he mentions in his note looks abandoned. There is no sign of your sister, nor anyone else for that matter."

"Would anyone have noticed you were there?"

Archibald flashed a rare grin, this one wry.

"You've hired the best, Your Grace. No one knew we were there."

"Good," Giles said with a nod. "What's the plan?"

Archibald opened his mouth to respond, but they both paused when there was a small scuffling outside the door. Giles sighed and looked over at Archibald, who was staring at him with a raised eyebrow and a slight curve to his lips.

"The plan," Archibald said slowly, "is to bait the kidnappers with more unsuspecting women. We'll throw them out into the middle of the meet-up and see what happens."

Despite the panic that was roiling in his stomach, threatening to rise and overwhelm him, Giles couldn't help a slight smirk as the noise at the door paused. As silently as he could, Giles rose from his chair and, in one swift motion, opened the door.

Which sent Prudence and Emma tumbling into the room.

"Giles!" Prudence protested. "That hurt!"

"Serves you right for eavesdropping."

"We are just concerned," Emma said, taking the hand that Giles held out to both of them and rising to her feet a slight bit more gracefully than Prudence, who was still grumbling. "We wouldn't have to eavesdrop if you would just tell us the plan to recover Juliana."

Giles looked back at Archibald and tilted his head to the door.

"Perhaps we best finish this conversation in the drawing room."

Archibald eyed him with a gaze that seemed to question

his control over his family, but Giles didn't care at the moment — he would exert that control once Juliana was returned.

When they had finally settled in the drawing room, surrounded by the Remington females and one Lady Emma, they continued the conversation.

"My men are in place," Archibald said, directing his comments to Giles. "See if you can entice the kidnappers to meet with you outside the house. If not, we will be waiting near the windows and doors. It remains your responsibility to determine what it is they are trying to accomplish."

"What if Juliana isn't there?" Giles asked. He didn't want to think of it, but they had to be prepared.

"Then we will let one or two of them get away, and we will follow them," Archibald said. "We best go now."

Giles nodded as he stood. He had dressed tonight in as dark of colors as he owned, all black and navy so that he didn't make an easy target.

He and Archibald had made it to the door before he turned around and looked at the worried faces of the women who stared at him.

"Do not worry. I'll take care of this," he said, concerned by their apparent lack of trust in him. "And whatever you do," he added. "Stay here. Archibald has men watching the house, so you are safest here. Do you understand?" He leveled the last question at Prudence and Emma.

They nodded, but Giles didn't like the way Emma was biting her lip in that way of hers that usually meant she was hiding something.

But there was nothing he could do except repeat himself as he walked through the door.

"Stay here." He paused before adding, "We'll be back."

* * *

EMMA AND PRUDENCE tried to do as Giles had said — they truly did.

It only took five minutes of alternating between sitting in the drawing room, pacing the floor, and staring out the window before Emma'd had about enough.

The duchess and her mother had promptly retired, although they made Emma and Prudence promise to wake them with news. Prudence had walked her mother to her bedroom, returning to tell Emma that she had made sure her mother drank a sleeping potion before bed to calm her distraught nerves.

Lady Winchester had poured herself a good brandy and pulled out a book, saying she would not sleep until Giles and Juliana were home. Emma believed that would be true.

"What did your parents say to you being here so late?" Prudence asked.

"They don't typically notice when I've gone. I inform the housekeeper, who can keep them apprised of my where-abouts if they happen to ask, but it's not unusual for me to be here."

"Right," Prudence said with a nod, turning her face but not before Emma caught a glimpse of pity. "How long do you think Giles will be?"

"I have no idea," Emma said, lifting the curtain of the front room one more time, only to stare out into the dark, empty night once more. "It's already past midnight."

"Can you see any of Archibald's men?" Prudence asked, but Emma shook her head.

"No. They must be good at what they do." She crossed her arms over her chest. "How long do we sit here and wait for them?"

Prudence tapped her foot nervously. "Until they return."

"But—"

"I know, Emma, I want to go too, but we would only cause more trouble."

"I just…" Emma shook her head. "I just have a bad feeling. A feeling that we should go. You don't have to. You stay here. I'll go, and I will take one of Archibald's men with me. I won't be able to do anything, but perhaps they might need additional hands and at least we would have the element of surprise."

Prudence nodded resolutely, even as a slight bit of fear flashed in her eyes. "Very well. Let's go, then."

"Prudence—"

"You are not going alone and there is no way I can sit here and wait for you, too."

A twinge of guilt pinched at Emma, but she ignored it as her will to help Giles and Juliana overcame all else. "Do you have another carriage?"

"Yes. We should take the one without the family crest. But Emma, how will we know where to go?"

"I saw the note," Emma said with a slight shrug.

"And you remember?"

"I have a fairly good memory."

"Well, let us go see if we can convince a groom, a driver, and one of Archibald's men to go along with our scheme."

GILES TENTATIVELY STEPPED toward the dilapidated building. They had arrived half an hour early, and he'd had to restrain himself from rushing in to find his sister.

The boards on the side of the house were held together by a few lingering nails, and as the wind cut through his cloak, he shuddered to think of where Juliana had spent the day. Was she warm? Was she hungry? Was she—? No. He wouldn't think about it. He couldn't. He stomped a little too hard on the floorboard of the first step, cursing himself as he pushed the thought out of his mind. All he could do was get her back.

He wished he had a way to communicate with Archibald, to know if he could see any signs of movement in or around the house. Giles was somewhat comforted to know that Archibald was nearby, but besides the other men's proximity, Giles was alone in this, going in without any idea of what he would be facing.

When he reached the door, he lifted his hand, unsure whether he should knock or just enter, but the decision was taken away from him when it swung open in front of him — revealing only blackness inside.

"Who's there?" he called into the darkness, but he was greeted with nothing — no sounds, no movement, not even a flicker of light.

He tried to wait until his eyes adjusted so that he could, at the very least, make out shadows in the room.

Somehow, he could sense, however, that there was someone waiting for him — if he was a betting man, there was most certainly someone standing either behind the door or in the room beyond. Whether Juliana was actually here, well, that was another story.

Not being a stupid man, he decided that he was best to walk away from the house to hopefully draw out whoever was awaiting him. He took one step backward, and then another, the heel of his boot causing the board beneath it to creak.

That's when he heard it.

"Giles!"

His heart skipped a beat.

"Juliana!" he practically roared, before he forgot all of his previous concerns and rushed inside.

Which was when the gun went off.

CHAPTER 9

"*A*rchibald and the duke will have my 'ide for this," the man muttered from outside the carriage window. Emma hadn't thought they would ever be able to convince him to accompany them, but when she told him that he would have to physically prevent them from leaving the house and he might as well join them rather than allowing them to go alone, he had finally relented.

He had sat up top with an equally reluctant driver, telling him to stop when they were a few houses away from the address. He had been to the site earlier, so he knew where to go but refused to allow them any closer.

"This is nearly as terrible as sitting at the house," Emma complained to Prudence, who was looking rather green. Prudence typically only ventured into the unknown when Juliana drew her there.

"Except that we're in danger here," Prudence said before swallowing hard, and Emma nodded in agreement.

"I suppose that's true."

"Mr. Pip?" Emma whispered through the window. "Can you see anything that's happening?"

"The duke is standing on the front steps. Our men are watching him from various locations but are all hidden. The door opened. The duke has stepped forward." He paused. "He's moving backward. Now—"

He was cut off by the gunshot. Prudence gave a shriek as Emma nearly jumped off her seat.

"Stay inside," The man who introduced himself only as Pip hushed as the horses whinnied. As much as she knew that they should be turning around and racing for home as fast as possible, Emma couldn't help the overwhelming fear that told her to stay as close to the situation as possible. Fear for Juliana, and fear for Giles. Why she cared so much if something happened to him, she had no idea. It must be because he was Juliana's brother, she told herself, but as she gripped Prudence's hand, she couldn't help but acknowledge the truth.

She wanted Giles to be safe because she cared for him.

"What is happening now?" Emma demanded to Pip, who was pacing back and forth beside the carriage.

"Our men have gone in. A few are still outside the perimeter. It looks like—someone is coming out. Our men. They are carrying someone in their arms. And—it looks like a woman is with them. She's walking."

Emma and Prudence exchanged a look. "Juliana!"

Sensing that the danger had passed, Emma pushed open the carriage door and started down the stairs, even as Pip protested that she must stay within.

"The danger has passed, Mr. Pip, has it not?" Emma asked, feeling sorry for him for a moment as she paused at the bottom of the stairs.

"I suppose," he said, wiping the sweat off his brow, even though the weather was as chilled as could be on a May night near London. "Looks like anyone who could have been a threat is gone."

"We shall be careful," Emma said, before she and Prudence, with Pip following, raced down the road toward the front path of the house that was now filled with men who must be Archibald's.

"Juliana!" she shouted when her friend came into view, and Juliana broke away from Mr. Archibald and ran toward Emma and Prudence with a cry until the three of them had their arms encircled around one another as tears began to run down Emma's face. It wasn't until she pulled back slightly that she realized all three of them were equally affected.

"Oh, Juliana, I'm so glad you are all right," Emma said. "You *are* all right, are you not? Oh, please, say—"

"I'm fine, I'm fine," Juliana said, heaving a huge sigh. "I'm shaken, but I'm fine."

"What happened?" Prudence asked, but before Juliana could say anything, Emma caught motion out of the corner of her eye. Fear gripping her heart, she turned to see that it was Giles, now lying on the ground as Mr. Archibald knelt at his side.

Emma couldn't have said later how she moved there nor how quickly, but one moment she was with her friends, and the next she was kneeling behind Giles, lifting his head to rest on the soft fabric of her skirts as she cradled it in her lap.

"What's wrong with him?" she demanded to Mr. Archibald, who was running his hands over Giles, ripping off his jacket to look beneath.

"I'm not sure," the detective muttered. "I thought he was fine. There was a gunshot, but I thought it missed him. Must have—bloody hell. Excuse me, my lady."

Emma waved away the apology as she leaned over with a gasp. When Mr. Archibald had pulled away Giles' jacket to reveal the shirt and waistcoat underneath, there, on the white of his linen shirt, red was spreading out like a spilled glass of wine.

Mr. Archibald ripped open the shirt from the middle, startling Emma, who was now surrounded by Juliana and Prudence on either side, Prudence sniffing while Juliana had one — very dirty — hand wrapped around Emma's arm in a tight grasp.

"He should be fine," Mr. Archibald was saying, but Emma nearly didn't hear him as she couldn't stop staring at Giles' face in front of her, his eyes closed, his skin pale.

"He was shot," Emma finally said, looking up at Mr. Archibald in desperation, praying that he was all right.

"Looks like it was more of a graze," Mr. Archibald said, even as Giles stirred.

"Did we get the bastards?" he muttered, before his eyes fluttered open, only to stare up into Emma's — although he didn't have much choice, from the way she was leaning over top of him and filling his vision.

"What are you doing here?"

He pushed himself off her lap and into a sitting position, seeing Prudence on the other side. "Pru, what in the—"

His breath then came out in a rush as he saw his other sister there, whole and presumably in one piece.

"Oh, Jules," he said, before turning toward her, the motion causing him to let out a painful groan as he did so.

"Perhaps do not move," Emma suggested with a grimace.

"Right," he muttered as his sister leaned over him instead, taking his hands in hers as her eyes filled with worry.

"Giles, thank you for coming for me. I wish I was able to somehow send word for you not to follow the note, for it was all a trap. I tried to tell you as you were coming through the door, but I'm afraid I only made it worse."

"You did," Mr. Archibald muttered from the other side of

her. "Had you not called out, His Grace could have led the attackers outside."

"No," Giles shook his head firmly, his lips set in a line. "It was the right thing to do, Jules, for they could have killed you otherwise. Who were they?"

"I don't know," she said, lifting her hands with desperate helplessness. "Their faces were covered, and I had the sense they were hired by someone else as one man didn't seem to have any idea what he was doing."

Mr. Archibald let out a grunt as Giles slowly rose to his feet. "What a waste of time."

"My sister was found alive and unharmed," Giles said, following gingerly, obviously doing his best not to utilize any of the outstretched hands from his sisters or Emma, although he winced as he must have pulled at his injury when he stood up. "I would say that we achieved our aim."

"Except that we're no closer to discovering the threat and none of you are safe," Mr. Archibald said before he walked a few steps away to where his men were awaiting his instruction.

"We should get home," Prudence said, looking around them, obviously still ill-at-ease. "We can decide what to do from there."

"How did you get here?" Giles asked, his voice deeper and lower than usual and Emma had a feeling that they were going to hear a great deal more on the fact that they had followed him.

"We took the carriage without the crest," Emma said before Prudence could answer. "Please don't blame Pru. I convinced her to come." Giles eyes narrowed further, and Emma felt the need to defend herself. "We had one of Mr. Archibald's men accompany us and we stayed away from the meeting place. We just—"

She was suddenly overwhelmed by emotion as she looked

to first Giles and then Juliana, and when her voice broke slightly, Juliana took pity on her.

"We'll discuss this at home, shall we?" Juliana said with a nod.

They looked toward the waiting carriages as Mr. Archibald rejoined them with orders.

"We believe it would be best that we have a few men accompany Lady Juliana and Lady Prudence. I will ride with them to ensure nothing goes amiss." He turned to Giles. "Your Grace, if you are comfortable in taking the other carriage home, my men will follow you as well. I'd suggest you come with us, but you shall need more room to lie flat with that wound."

Giles' jaw tightened. "I would prefer not to leave my sisters."

"They are in the best of hands. I promise you that," Archibald said. "And forgive me, Your Grace, but you are not in much of a state to look after them."

They began to walk toward the carriages, boots crunching over the gravel at their feet, as Emma looked around her, wondering just what she was supposed to do.

"Shall I go with Lady Juliana, then?" Emma asked, twisting her hands in front of her.

"There will be more room with His Grace," Archibald said before shutting the carriage door, blocking her from her friends, and Emma turned around to find Giles staring at her and then the closed carriage door.

"Never thought I'd be ordered about by a commoner," he said, but despite his annoyance, he was listing slightly to one side and Emma realized that she was going to have to be the one to get him safely home.

"Let's go inside, then, shall we?" she asked, and before he could respond, she stepped beneath his arm to allow him to lean on her. She could tell he was trying to resist as he began to stumble toward the carriage, but eventually even his stubbornness couldn't make up for the weakness that had filled him, and he let her help him up the steps until he flopped down on the seat without much of the grace he had been blessed with.

He closed his eyes as he ran a hand through his hair and over his face in a gesture that Emma had come to recognize as that which he did when he wasn't entirely sure of how to handle the situation.

The carriage swayed as Archibald's men climbed on top, and Emma finally allowed herself to relax slightly, knowing that, for now at least, they were all safe and in good hands.

"What you did tonight was very brave, Your Grace," she said tentatively, breaking the tense silence that had filled the carriage.

"It wasn't brave," he said, his eyes still closed. "It was desperate. If Juliana hadn't been there, or—"

He stopped, obviously unable to speak the worst, and Emma moved across the seat, gently lifting his head and placing it in her lap once more. His eyes flew open and met hers with confused curiosity, but he didn't protest or move away. Feeling the need to do something to ease his pain and concern, she began to stroke his slightly too long hair back away from his brow, running her hands through its silkiness. She swallowed hard, knowing that this was wrong, that she had no claim to this man, that she was taking a liberty that he would likely never have otherwise allowed — but it felt right, it felt good, and even though she knew it was far too forward, far too brazen, she prayed that he would suspend propriety for this night that was nothing any of them would ever have expected to experience.

He looked up once more, meeting her eyes, and Emma couldn't have said how long they sat there, staring at one another in the dim light as the carriage rolled over the bumpy roads back into London.

When one bump particularly rocked her, Emma had to grip tightly onto Giles' shoulders to keep him from rolling off her lap, and he grimaced slightly as he reached up and covered one of her hands with his.

"I'm still annoyed with you," he said, his voice in the carriage almost surprising after the silence. "But I do thank you for caring — for me and for my sisters. You are like family to us."

She nodded, looking up and away from him as the slight bit of unease filled her. She was like family to them, this was true, and yet… she couldn't help the yearning to be more to him. It was ridiculous, she knew. She was certainly not the type of woman he needed. That much was made clear. He was the brother of her dearest friend, and she was well aware that he looked at her like a little sister.

Besides that, he was a rake, she reminded herself. A man who fulfilled his needs with women who were much more available to him, women he wouldn't have to wed were he caught with them.

"We shall have to make sure that no one knows we were alone together in here," she murmured, speaking her thoughts aloud, and his eyes widened slightly as his nostrils flared, as though the idea hadn't occurred to him.

"I would say that tonight is a night in which we can suspend all rules and expectations that would normally be placed upon us," he murmured, looking up at her.

"That is fair," she said, as her heart started to beat much more rapidly at the intensity of his gaze. There was something in his eyes. Something she couldn't quite describe, but that her body seemed to recognize before her mind did.

He surprised her by pushing himself up, until the middle of his back was upon her lap, his shoulders and elbows braced on the side wall of the carriage beside him. His head was level with hers, the ocean blue of his eyes staring into hers until they dropped — to her mouth.

Before Emma quite realized what was happening, he leaned in, and pressed his lips against hers.

CHAPTER 10

One moment he was staring into the sea green of her eyes, lost in their depths and the comfort she offered.

She must have bewitched him somehow with her gaze — that was the only explanation for why, in the next moment, he found himself being drawn forward, until he was but a breath away, and then his lips descended, ever so slowly, upon hers.

He closed his eyes as their plush softness welcomed him like a pillow he would lay his head upon after coming home, and for a brief moment a bolt of panic shot through him at just how right this felt — but then she was kissing him back and the panic fled, to be replaced by a need for her so great that it overwhelmed all else.

The moment their lips touched, his entire body — which had been feeling weaker than he could ever remember — seemed to catch fire. Her mouth parted, likely without her even realizing what she was doing, from the surprise of his touch.

But Giles found that he didn't care how or why she

opened for him — just that she did. Somewhere, in the back of his mind, he knew she was an innocent, that this could very well be her first kiss.

It shocked him how much the thought of someone else kissing her caused a possessive fury to rise within him, as he was suddenly consumed with the need to be the first — if not the first to kiss her, then the first to show her just what a true kiss was.

He was expecting her to be shocked, to be uncertain enough to allow him to do as he pleased, which he did as he swept his tongue into her mouth, tasting her, branding her, accepting all that she offered.

And then he was the one who was taken off guard when she leaned in, took the lapels of his jacket in her fists, and kissed him back with all the direct straightforwardness she spoke and acted with.

Giles would have thought a kiss with an innocent like Emma would be a slow exploration, a meeting in which they would learn more about one another.

But instead of a slow burn, this was a wildfire.

He should have expected it of her, should have known that she never did anything tentatively or halfway. She was inexperienced, that much was obvious — but what she lacked there, she more than made up for in her enthusiasm.

For a moment it was as though she was going to take charge, but Giles was having none of that. He would take comfort from her, but in this? He would be the one to show her what it was to be kissed.

While his left arm stayed clenched tightly against his side, his other reached out and pulled her close. Off-balance, she fell against him, and while he grunted at the pressure it placed on his wound, it wasn't enough to make him stop. One would have thought that all of the occur-rences of the evening would have cooled his ardour, but instead he found himself as hard as a rock for her, and he shifted so that she wouldn't realize exactly how much he wanted her. She may be enthusiastic, but he had a feeling that a true show of his desire might be a bit much for her to take in.

Slowly, reluctantly, he gentled the kiss, until it was just his lips on hers, which was somehow more soul-baring than the kiss itself.

When he finally released her, leaning back against the seat once more, she was blinking rapidly, as though she could hardly believe what had just happened.

And truth be told, neither could he.

Her lips were pink and swollen, her eyes glassy, unfocused, covered in a haze of desire that made him want to kiss her again.

Except he knew better.

"Emma, I—I must apologize," he said, trying to form coherent words from his muddled thoughts. "It's been a night, and I—you were here, and you seemed open to it, and so I—"

"That's why you kissed me. I was here."

"Yes, I—no. No, that is not it at all."

Oh, he was making a mess of this, of that he was well aware. She was looking at him now with murder in her gaze and he had a feeling that he had said exactly the wrong thing, which was not at all the norm for him. Usually, he knew which words would charm a woman, to have her coming back for more.

But Emma was different. For he knew her, unlike the other women whose names and faces faded for they had meant nothing at all but a warm bed to pass the time in.

"I think this has all gone terribly wrong," he said, trying to amend the damage, but it seemed he was only making things worse, for at that she narrowed her eyes even further, if that were possible, as she pushed him off her and tried to slide away over to the other seat.

"Well, in that case, we will make sure that this never happens again, then, shall we? For it was all some *horrible mistake*."

She said the words with such vehemence that Giles was well aware he had completely mucked up this exchange, but he wasn't entirely sure where his error had been.

"Emma—"

But the carriage had come to a halt, and she was already standing, the door open and one foot out.

"It is *Lady Emma* to you, Your Grace," she retorted, leaving him to sit up with a groan as one of the lucky men outside helped her down the stairs.

* * *

EMMA REALIZED that her little tirade in the carriage had likely done nothing but prove a point — that she was the immature friend of Giles' little sister.

But she had been so overcome by the entire evening.

That had been the most epic, amazing, incredible, heart-stopping kiss of her life.

It had also been the *only* kiss of her life, but she could hardly imagine how one could be any better than that. She had not enjoyed the fact that the duke was a rake, but the rake certainly knew how to kiss a woman, that was for certain.

Then he had gone and ruined it all by first apologizing and then telling her how terribly wrong it had all been, that it had only happened because it had been an emotional night.

As though any woman who had been with him in the carriage would have been subjected to the same treatment.

Not that it was a particular hardship.

He would have to venture out of the carriage alone, wounded or not. He could rely on the men he paid to help him, for Emma most certainly was no longer interested in doing so.

Despite her annoyance, however, she could not help the tingle he had left upon her lips, nor the desire that had pooled in her stomach and then had descended between her legs. She had heard tales before of what it was like to want a man. Whispered words in a ballroom corner. Secrets told between women of what went on behind closed doors. Her mother had never been particularly forthcoming, but as the sisters of a rake, Juliana and Prudence had managed to learn a few things, and any questions they had were answered by their grandmother, of all people.

Emma had been shocked, until Lady Winchester had regaled the tale of her own first night of marriage as an uneducated virgin whose husband had not provided a great deal of explanation before he had taken her to the marriage bed having incorrectly assumed her mother would have yielded those details. She declared it was an experience she would wish upon no one and had vowed that any of her female descendants would be properly prepared. She did finish with the caveat that her explanation was perhaps not something to be shared with the duchess.

While Lady Winchester had provided the basic information, she had been rather vague on just how a woman should react, leaving Emma to wonder whether she was wickedly wanton for her desire for more — particularly outside of the duke's marriage bed, a place where Emma would most certainly never find herself.

"Emma!" Juliana called out to her as she stepped into the room.

After the butler allowed her entrance, Emma had made her way to the drawing room, where she was told that the ladies Juliana and Prudence were waiting. She was not surprised to find Lady Winchester sitting there in her chair before the fire, bedclothes and wrapper around her and all.

"We all made it back, I see," Emma said, taking a seat next to Juliana. "I'm surprised you are not off to bed already."

"I wanted to make sure that Giles was all right before I did," she said. "I am most particularly exhausted, however."

"I cannot imagine what you have gone through," Emma murmured, practically bursting with questions, just as Giles filled the entrance of the room. He shot an unreadable look her way, and Emma found herself biting her lip as she considered what had just occurred between them — and prayed that Juliana wouldn't notice anything.

Oh goodness. Her first kiss and she wouldn't be able to tell Juliana about it. How could she? Juliana would either be horrified or would be planning their wedding in order to make Emma her sister in truth. While Emma herself should be thinking of no one *except* Juliana in this moment.

"I have many questions for you, Jules," he said, not sitting but leaning against the mantel over the fireplace. He was likely worried that if he sat down, he would never stand up again.

"But they shall have to wait until tomorrow. Let us all get some sleep, and we will decide what to do in the morning."

Juliana stood, and for the first time Emma noticed just how torn and tattered her friend's dress was.

"But what about your wound, Giles? Should we call for a surgeon?" Juliana asked.

"No." He shook his head, turning away from her. "Absolutely not. I shall have my valet dress it and it will be perfectly fine. Archibald was right. It just grazed my side."

"You did faint," Emma couldn't help but point out, and Giles' head whipped around so quickly toward her that she was worried he would fall over again.

"It was nothing," he said. "Just a bit of a knock to the head on my way out."

"Pardon me?" Juliana practically shrieked, causing Giles to wince once more, as Emma sighed inwardly. A head injury would explain why he had kissed her, that was for certain.

"I am fine, Jules, truly," he said, exhaustion seeming to overtake him. "Now off to bed with the lot of you. We will discuss everything in the morning. Lady Emma, you might as well stay the night."

"We already had the extra room made up for her," Lady Winchester said from the corner, and Giles eyes softened for his grandmother, which also caused compassion within Emma, to know how much he cared for her. Lady Winchester stood and walked over to Giles as the women began to filter out of the room and up to bed. Emma paused in the doorway, wondering if she should linger and speak to Giles about what had transpired in the carriage — or at least apologize for her response.

But then she heard Lady Winchester's, "I'm proud of you, my boy," and she found that she had to run off before any of them saw the tears that filled her eyes.

CHAPTER 11

*G*iles hadn't lied — he had intended on asking the valet to help him with his bandages. He just hadn't considered that the man might be unable to stand the sight of blood.

Rogers had taken one look at the bloody bandages and had turned so pale that Giles thought the valet was soon going to be the one lying prone on the floor.

"Oh, for goodness' sake," he muttered. "If you bring me what I need, Rogers, I will do it myself."

Which left him now struggling to turn far enough to properly wrap the linen around himself. He had never better understood a woman's need for a lady's maid.

He grunted and groaned, but for the life of him, could not properly turn to grasp the other side of the bandage. By this point, he was sure the rest of the house was sleeping, and he was pondering whether he should just leave it as it was, but there was a trickle of blood that wouldn't stop, and he was worried that it might worsen as he slept. Just as he came to the decision that he was going to have to wake Prudence, there was a soft knock at the door. He stalked toward it.

"Rogers, I told you, I will not—" He flung open the door. "Oh. Lady Emma."

She stood in the hall, hands clasped in front of her, uncertainty on her face. She was dressed in what he was sure was one of Juliana's chaste high-necked white nightrails with a deep pink wrapper cinched overtop, looking like a birthday present all wrapped up and waiting for him.

"What are you doing?" he couldn't help but ask as he turned around and reached for his banyan, hanging it over his shoulders but leaving it gaping open so he could still access his wound.

"I heard you moaning and groaning as if someone was stabbing you in your gunshot wound but then it stopped, and I figured I had best come make sure you were still alive." Her words came out quickly, rushed as if she was trying to make sure that he was aware as soon as possible that no other reason could entice her to his bedroom. She blinked once, twice, as it seemed her gaze couldn't quite reach his face — instead, she was staring right in front of her at his bare chest, gaping between the lapels of his banyan as he held strips of linen against his wound to keep it from bleeding.

Despite the ache in his side and the knowledge that he had already insulted her once today, he couldn't help but tease her a bit more.

"You haven't come to truly compromise me, then, have you?" he asked, one side of his lips turning up into a grin when she glared at him and finally met his eyes.

"If I wanted to force you into marriage, Your Grace, I could already do so with our indiscretion in the carriage, could I not?"

"Touché, my lady," he couldn't help but acknowledge, surprised at himself when the panic that should have taken hold at the thought of a woman trapping him into marriage didn't seem to register.

She took a step backward. "Well, now that I have seen you are alive—"

"Since you are here," he said, holding up the bandages in his hand, "do you suppose you could wrap my wound? I cannot seem to do it myself and Rogers — my valet — nearly fell over at the sight of it. I realize it is not exactly something for a lady to *see* let alone do, but—"

"It's fine," she said, holding out a hand to him. "Pass it here."

He set the bandages into her hand and stepped back into the room. She looked from one side of the hall to the next before she followed him inside, shutting the door behind her. He looked at her with one eyebrow raised in question, and she shrugged.

"Servants talk. If they knew I was in here with you in the early hours of the morning—"

"Right." His mind was muddled from the knock to his head, and, it seemed, anything that came to Lady Emma and rational thought.

"Sit," she commanded, and he took a seat on the edge of the bed, closing his eyes for a moment as he attempted to control himself, for her proximity in his bedroom was causing all types of improper thoughts to fill his mind.

Funny, he had known the woman since she was still in the nursery and he was a boy about to leave for school, and he had looked at her as nothing but a child ever since. Even over the past year, since his return, he had spent a good deal of time in her presence but had never really *seen* her. But now that he had… he couldn't seem to *un*see the woman she had become.

Her hands were soft, her touch light, and when Giles snuck a quick look up at her face, her nose was wrinkled in concentration, her tongue caught between her teeth as she focused on the task in front of her.

She attempted to hold his banyan back, out of the way, but it kept falling forward and covering the wound.

"You'll have to remove this," she said, looking up at him, and when their eyes caught, he had to force himself to breathe, as he was so taken aback by the heat that hung in the air between them.

He didn't release her gaze as he shrugged out of the garment, didn't shrink from her touch as she reached out and with clear determination pushed the fabric over his shoulders until it slipped onto the bed in a pool of silk behind him.

How she remained so unaffected, Giles had no idea — especially when his own blood was so heated he thought that she must be able to hear his heart beating from where she stood beside him.

But then he saw the bob of the long column of her throat as she swallowed hard, and he realized that perhaps she wasn't as unaffected as she let on.

"Turn," she murmured as she bent her head to pick up a strip of linen. "I think I should clean some of the blood away first."

"You do not have to—"

She ignored him as she dipped a piece of linen in the water basin and then began to wipe away the blood. She was gentle at first, but when the dried blood stuck, she pushed a little harder and Giles sucked in a breath.

"Sorry," she muttered, but he shook his head.

"It's fine," he said. "Do as you need to."

She nodded, set her jaw, and went to work as he sat there with his eyes closed, breathing in and out from between his teeth as he tried to keep his face impassive. If nothing else, at least the tugging on the wound helped him forget the desire that roared up within him every time he was around her.

"There, that's the best I can do, I believe," she eventually said before sitting back on her heels.

He grunted. "How does it look?"

"You'll live," she said, smiling up at him.

He reached out a hand to help her to her feet. When she took it, heat sizzled between their palms. She gravitated toward him, leaning in slightly, until the sound of footsteps in the hall had her jumping away. Giles put a finger against his lips, knowing there was no one who should be out of bed who would have any reason to come into his room. The footsteps grew louder but soon receded, and Emma let out a breath.

"I suppose I best wrap this now," she whispered, and he nodded, not trusting himself to say anything, for if he opened his mouth, it might be to draw her in closer to him once more, or to tell her what he was truly feeling toward her at the moment.

She placed one piece of linen on the wound, and as she leaned over him, a citrusy scent that reminded him of summer wafted up from her unbound hair. If he didn't know better, he would have said that the smell went into his nostrils and straight through to his loins.

"Can you hold this?" she asked, and he nodded, not trusting himself to say anything. As he held it, she took the longer strip of linen and used one hand to hold it against his abdomen, causing Giles to feel infinitely grateful that he still maintained his membership at Jackson's. She used the other hand to wrap the linen around his body, leaning into him, her arms coming around him as she stretched it over his back.

Giles might be a gentleman in name, but his reputation spoke otherwise.

And it was his reputation that took over now.

"Emma," he murmured as she let out a grunt while trying

to reach the fabric. On some women the sound might have been embarrassing, but coming from her it was both alluring and adorable at the same time.

"Yes? Oh, I've got it. Thank goodness."

"Yes, thank goodness," he murmured, tilting his chin down to stare at the crown of her head as she tied the strip. She leaned back ever so slightly away from him as she looked down as though to admire her work.

"That should be satisfactory," she said before looking up at him, a small smile playing on her lips.

That was her first mistake.

* * *

EMMA WAS WELL aware that this was the height of impropriety. At this point, they were certainly tempting fate by the number of times they had been alone together in circumstances that could have led to a lifetime together instead of just a few moments.

But how could she say no to a duke who had obviously humbled himself just by asking for help? In some ways, she was aware that this vulnerability was a rarity for him, and she couldn't see how she could deny his request.

She had been well aware as she dressed his wound, however, that she should avoid looking him in the eyes, for that would only leave herself at risk of falling into their depths and never being able to surface.

Her second mistake? Not drawing back when she recognized his predatory look when she finally had met them.

The moment she had seen that tanned, glorious strip of skin peeking out from the opening of his banyan, she had grown so hot she wondered how he didn't feel it radiating off her against his bare skin just inches away. Then he had lost the robe entirely and she thought that she — a woman who had never once fainted in her entire life — was about to fall to the floor.

Fortunately, she had managed to rally herself and dress his wound. She had thought she was safe, that she had kept herself from falling. That was her final mistake.

If someone had told her that passion could leave one person's body to join with a second, she would have told them that they were losing their sanity. But then that was exactly what had happened between them, and as the passion invaded, her senses escaped.

"Your Grace, I—"

"Giles," he said, his voice a caress in itself. "I believe we have become close enough for you to call me Giles."

"G-Giles," she stammered, but then completely forgot what it was she had been about to say to him.

"You should go," he said instead.

"I should."

Yet she remained where she was, her feet rooted to the floor, her body but a few inches from his.

She couldn't have said who moved first. But one moment they were standing there staring at one another, and the next they were fused together — lips, chests, oh goodness, hips, thighs — she couldn't have said where one of them began and the other one ended.

Emma hoped that she had learned something from that first kiss, and this time he didn't have to coax her to open up to him, for she did that entirely of her own accord. His mouth had captured hers, and she tasted the brandy he must have used to wash away some of the pain from his wound. Emma thought she had been hot before, but now she was on fire as his lips moved over hers, his hands ran up and down her body, over the silk of the thin wrapper she was wearing until one came to cup her bottom and she let out a little yelp into his mouth as he held her against him, making her very aware of what he was currently feeling and how dangerous a situation she had now found herself in.

And yet she couldn't bring herself to push him away. Not yet.

They kissed with a desperation that she felt deep within her soul, but this time, she wasn't completely oblivious to the world around her. This time, she remembered that while this was her first — make that second — kiss, he had kissed an infinite number of women before. He had only chosen her tonight because he was too incapacitated to go out and find another woman to spend the night with.

That thought was finally enough to have her pushing away from him, her hands coming to rest on that glorious chest, above the abdomen she had been trying to ignore since she had knocked on his door.

"You cannot — *we* cannot do this," she said firmly, her words as much for herself as they were for him.

He arched a thick brow at her. "I do not recall forcing you to do anything."

"That is true," she said but continued on. "But we should not be here together. We should not have the opportunity to do this. You are—you do not even care that it is me."

His expression became bemused. "What is that supposed to mean?"

"That I could be anyone — that it doesn't matter to you if you are with me or another nameless woman who would bare herself before you. Just because I am here with you in my nightclothes does not mean—"

He stood, causing Emma to swallow and take a step back. He was so tall, his height so perfect for her, that she was overwhelmed by his size and his very *male*ness.

"There is something I need you to understand," he said hotly.

She nodded but crossed her arms over her chest in a very futile motion of self-defense.

"If I did not want you," he said, his words slow and measured, "I would have sent you back out this door without any inkling that there was even a possibility. Do you understand me?"

She managed another nod before he continued. She must look like a malfunctioning puppet.

"Heaven help me, but it is *you* that has crawled her way under my skin, it is *you* that I want in my bed despite my better judgement, and there is no one else but *you* that I would want with me right now. Understand?"

Emma was well aware that if there were any words that should sway her, it should be romantic, poetic words that would speak to her soul.

Yet somehow his crude declaration was all she needed.

She let out a growl of frustration and meant to whirl around and storm through the door. She truly did.

But instead, she was lifting her hands to his face and pulling him down for another kiss. The next thing she knew, his hands were beneath her bottom, lifting her up, and it seemed like the most natural thing in the world to wrap her legs around him, despite that it meant his rather hard — what should she call it? Lady Winchester had never shared that much — was fit against her, pressing on a part of her that seemed more than willing to accept him.

While Emma wasn't entirely sure what to do, her body seemed to know as she moved slightly against him, and he let out a groan as he turned around and lay her down on the bed.

She looked up at him, her eyes hard on his as she needed him to understand something.

"I am not another title-seeking woman who is trying to trap you into marriage."

"You have made that clear," he said with a low chuckle.

"No one can know about this — about us. Especially not Juliana."

"You would be the only one who would tell her."

"Good," she said, releasing a breath, but he caught the sigh as his lips covered hers again, and she, quite embarrassingly, felt herself moaning into his mouth.

Emma couldn't have said how long he kissed her — she only knew that she was losing herself to his touch. When one of his huge hands rose to cup her breast, his thumbs splaying over her nipples, she arched up into him, begging for more without using words. He answered her with his right hand, which came up to cup her other breast, until he shocked her by bending his head and unbuttoning the top of her night rail just enough that he could lift one of her breasts through the opening.

Emma moaned at the exquisiteness of his touch, even as a niggling voice at the back of her mind questioned what was happening, what she was doing, whether she should allow him to continue.

But he made the decision for her as he suddenly pulled back so quickly that she was left nearly frozen from the loss of his heat.

He didn't completely step back from her — no, he was leaning down and buttoning up the top of her borrowed night rail — but when that was finished, he was putting the dressing gown back on, tightening it around himself as he ran one hand through his hair.

"You have to go," he said, in a way that made Emma nearly shiver at the harshness of his words.

"I—"

"Go. Now." His eyes were hard, dark, and Emma suddenly felt utterly wanton at how she had behaved.

Filled with shame, she did as he said. She fled.

CHAPTER 12

*E*mma wondered if anyone would notice if she snuck out of the house before they gathered for breakfast. At least they wouldn't be having an extravagant breakfast such as they would in the country, but she had a feeling that Juliana, at least, would question why she hadn't stayed.

She could hardly tell her friend it was because she had behaved like a harlot, parading in front of the duke in her nightclothes and then had been unable to keep her hands off him when she had seen him without a shirt. One sight of a naked — although rather perfect — man, and she was throwing herself at him as if he was the only chance she would ever have to know a masculine touch.

Which could be true.

She also knew that her curiosity would get the better of her if she didn't remain to hear just what, exactly, had transpired when Juliana had been taken. She was aware that it likely wasn't quite as terrible as she had made it out to be in her imaginings and thought it best to replace her suspicions with truth instead of fiction of her own creation.

Perhaps she would be lucky, and the duke would stay

abed long enough for her to leave, so that she wouldn't have to see him again, at least not so soon. Emma certainly had never known him to appear at breakfast any other time she had stayed over in the household, after he had likely spent the night carousing. Today certainly wouldn't be any different.

Or so she thought, until he appeared at the table a few minutes later.

The women in the family were already there. While Emma was aware that Lady Winchester and the duchess typically broke their fast in their own chambers, today was obviously an anomaly after all they had been through over the past few days.

They all looked up in surprise when Giles walked into the room.

"Good morning," he said in a surprisingly robust voice, and Emma found she couldn't look up at him as her face immediately filled with heat. She prayed that Juliana wouldn't look at her, for she would know in an instant that something was amiss. She had already asked Emma why she looked so tired, which had led to Emma feeling like a horrible friend, for it was Juliana's plight that should have kept her awake, not Giles' face — and hands.

"Giles!" Juliana said as she dropped her fork on her plate. "What are you doing?"

He furrowed his brow. "Having breakfast with the lovely women of my family."

"But you never have breakfast with us," Prudence said with a frown, obviously not entirely pleased at the change in routine.

"My sister has also never been taken and returned before," he answered smartly, which halted the comments from his siblings.

A knock sounded on the front door and the women all stopped, staring at one another.

"Who could that possibly be?" the duchess asked. Despite the events of the day before, she was obviously keen on maintaining the proper social customs. "It is before noon!"

"It is close to noon," Giles said wryly. "We had a rather late night. For many, the day is already halfway finished. That will be Matthew Archibald. I held him off as long as I could, but he has questions. I thought it would be best that Juliana tells us all the story at the same time, so she doesn't have to repeat herself."

Emma looked over at her friend, whose gaze was down on the table. She reached over and placed a hand on her arm. "Are you all right?" she asked softly, and Juliana nodded, although from the way she reached out and clutched her teacup, Emma had a feeling that she wasn't looking forward to re-living it all again.

As Giles predicted, the butler soon announced Matthew Archibald, who looked around at them all in the dining room rather uncomfortably.

"Archibald," Giles greeted him. "Take a seat, please. Have some breakfast if you'd like."

Mr. Archibald removed his hat and took the seat at the end of the table.

"Thank you, but I am fine. My apologies. I didn't mean to interrupt your meal."

"Not at all," Giles said, lifting his cup of coffee. He seemed at ease, but Emma had the feeling that most of it was a show, put on to try to convince the rest of them that everything was well. "I thought now would be the best time for Juliana to tell her tale."

Mr. Archibald nodded, and Emma couldn't help but feel sorry for him, for he was obviously not at all comfortable sitting at the dining table of a duke.

"How do the two of you fare today?" he asked Giles and Juliana, the latter of whom shrugged and said, "fine," briskly.

"Never better," Giles said dryly, and when Emma stole a peek at him, she immediately froze when he returned her stare. Before she could look away, he winked at her, and she choked on the sip of tea she had just taken. All at the table turned to her when she sputtered, and Giles couldn't hide his grin even behind his coffee cup. She glared at him before she looked around at the rest of the table.

"My apologies," Emma said once she had cleared her throat. "Please continue."

If nothing else, she had at least broken some of the tension. Giles simply said, "Juliana?" and all eyes turned to her. She had her hands fisted tightly in her lap, the only sign that she wasn't completely comfortable sharing with them all what had happened to her.

"I was on my way to meet Emma," she began. "I had left with my maid, Abigail, as I would any other day. We had just reached the end of the green when there was a commotion in front of one of the houses. We stopped to look, and a young boy came up to me. I somewhat recognized him. I believe he is one of the young ones in the neighborhood who holds horses and takes messages for coin. He asked me if I was Lady Juliana. I said I was. He told me that there was a litter of pups in distress around the corner and was told that I could help. I was fool enough to believe him."

Her cheeks turned pink as she looked down at that part of her story, and Emma's heart went out to her.

"There is no shame in having a good heart, Jules," she said softly, and Juliana nodded before she raised her head, a bit of strength returned in the set of her chin.

"Would it be in character for you to care about a litter of dogs?" Mr. Archibald asked, a notebook in front of him on the table despite the duchess' disapproving stare at the blatant conduct of business at her breakfast table.

"The girl would lie down in the middle of the road to

allow an animal with injury to cross," Lady Winchester said with a snort, but despite her words, her gaze upon her granddaughter was one of affection.

Mr. Archibald didn't seem to have an opinion on the subject.

"Then whoever arranged this knew you well enough to understand how to capture your attention," he said without expression. "Continue."

"I followed him," Juliana continued. "But the moment I stepped around the side of the building, my head was covered from behind and I was picked up and carried away. They must have been quick if Abigail didn't see anything. The next thing I knew, I was in a cart of some kind. It was just wood under my back, and I had enough room to stretch out, although my hands were tied. I was back there for, perhaps, a quarter of an hour before we stopped. I was lifted out but told to walk. The ground was uneven, soft, so perhaps we were out of London already. When the head covering was finally lifted, I was in a house and the one window was too dirty to see out, so I'm not sure where I was."

"What was the house like?" Archibald continued his questions.

"Furnished, but poorly. Ripped material on the furnishings, scratched wood, mismatched pieces."

"Did it look like someone actually lived there?"

"Perhaps, but not a family or anyone who had made it a home, if that makes sense."

"It does. Was anyone in the room with you?"

"Not at first," Juliana shook her head. "That was the worst part of it all. I had no idea where I was, what was happening, if I was going to be—to be—"

"You weren't," Emma murmured. "You're fine now."

"I know," Juliana said, although she lifted a hand to her

forehead. "I know."

Thankfully, Archibald gave her a moment before he asked her to continue. Emma stole a look at Giles and found that his expression, usually so light and amiable, had turned murderous.

Emma swallowed hard. There was so much she had thought to be true about Giles, and he had surprised her by proving her wrong time and again over the past few days. He was protective, intent on righting wrongs and keeping his family safe.

Not like the carefree rake she had thought him to be.

Emma couldn't help but watch him, even as Juliana spoke.

"Finally, a man arrived. It was dark and his face was covered. I didn't recognize him. He said nothing. He brought food and water for me and then left. He was the one who came and went, but he never said a word, no matter what I asked him. At one point, another man came into the room. He was dressed finer than the first man, but also had his face covered."

"Did he speak to you?" Archibald asked.

"He finally broke after I kept pestering him. He told me that I wasn't to be afraid, that if my brother did what was asked of him, I would be able to leave alive and unharmed."

"Did you feel threatened? Did you believe him?"

"I—" Juliana paused. "Do you know, it seemed to me that he was quite nervous himself. That he wasn't entirely looking forward to Giles' arrival, even though that was what he apparently wanted."

"Did he have any weapons?"

"No. The other man had had a pistol on him, however. I could see it in his belt."

"Did you try the doors?"

"Of course. There were two doors, both locked from the

outside," Juliana said. "The one window was too dirty to see through."

"How did they move you to the house where we found you?"

"The same way they transported me to the original house. Face covered, hands tied, in the back of a wagon. If I had to guess, I believe they took me through a back door, for we didn't walk far once within the house. They left me in a back room, but I could see the first man with the pistol waiting for you to walk in the front door, Giles. When I saw you standing there, framed in the doorway—"

Her voice broke as she looked down, and Emma squeezed her hand, even as her own heart restricted at just how close Giles had been to losing his life.

"I wasn't sure if I should have called your name or not," Juliana finally continued. "But I figured if I didn't warn you and you left, he would only have shot you in front of the house. I heard the shot, but you continued on to me, so I didn't realize that he actually grazed you with the bullet. That was an excellent punch, by the way."

"Thank you," Giles said with a nod.

"That's when you all came, and whoever was within the building left out the back once they realized that Giles wasn't alone," Juliana said, twining her fingers together and placing them on the table next to her plate of fruit and buns, which had only been half-touched.

"It's obvious that this was all some ploy to get to you, Your Grace," Mr. Archibald said, and Emma felt her heart hammering in her chest. Someone wanted Giles dead. Which made Emma extremely aware of how very much she would prefer that he remain alive. Mr. Archibald looked around the table. "Perhaps you and I should speak in your study?"

Lady Winchester harumphed from her side of the table. "You might as well say it all in front of us. The girls will only listen at the door anyway, and just because I am old does not mean that I cannot handle the truth. Elizabeth, can you hold yourself together to hear the rest of it?"

The duchess opened her mouth as if to tell her mother that she did not appreciate being spoken to as a child in front of the rest of them, but then the fight went out of her, and she nodded.

"Very well," Mr. Archibald said. "I haven't had enough time to properly look into the death of the former duke, but there is reason to believe that the same person who poisoned him wants you dead as well, Your Grace. Can you think of anyone who would substantially benefit if you were to pass on?"

Giles held his jaw tight, one fist on the table in front of him.

"Next in line for the title would be the son of my father's cousin, but Hemingway is a good chap. Not the sort to resort to anything of this manner and he has a title himself."

"Any enemies?"

"None that I can think of."

"Card games gone wrong? Husbands cuckolded?"

The duchess took exception to that comment. "Pardon me, Mr. Archibald, but—"

Giles looked a little green now. "Perhaps we *should* take this into my study."

If Emma wasn't mistaken, there was the hint of a smirk on Mr. Archibald's face. "Very well. Before we do, however, I have a suggestion for the entire family."

"Yes?"

"You should leave London. The danger is higher here in the city and I believe you would be far better away from here as we determine who took Lady Juliana and has it out for you."

"The Season has not yet finished!" the duchess protested,

but before Mr. Archibald could say anything, Lady Winchester had poked her with one long, bony finger.

"Do be as smart as I raised you to be, Elizabeth," she said, before leaning into Giles. "We should go to the country."

"Parliament is still in session," he hedged, and then jumped when his grandmother smacked his hand.

"You only attend half of the sessions, anyway!"

Giles shuffled in his seat like a scolded child. "Perhaps, but I am keen on—"

"Oh, for heaven's sake," Lady Winchester said. "We will go to Remington Estate for a week. We are fortunate that is only a half-day away. When all is cleared up here, we will return. Now, do go speak about the men who have it out for you, Giles, and we will begin our packing."

Emma had to cough to hide her snicker, even though Lady Winchester obviously appreciated it, for she looked to her with a nod and a twinkle in her eye.

Emma leaned over to Juliana. "You know I shall miss you, but it will be good to know that you are safe."

"Oh, but Emma, you must come with us!" Juliana said, her eyes wide and bright.

"I couldn't," Emma said, shaking her head.

"Whyever not?" Juliana said, tilting her head. "You have come with us so many times before, and what do you have keeping you here in London? Do not say your gardens, because I know you have Bernard to look after them for you."

Emma opened her mouth for a moment and then shut it again. For the truth, the reason she could not go was sitting at the end of the table, looking all handsome and disgruntled. She wondered what he thought about the possibility of her accompanying them. He was probably considering that at least she would help him pass the time while he was away from all of his other women.

Which was entirely the problem. For Emma knew that, deep within her, she wouldn't mind passing the time with him either.

Juliana tugged at her hands and Emma was reminded once more why going would be such a terrible idea. Giles was her best friend's brother, and she had no business in thinking of him in such a way — especially when one day he would belong to another. To a woman like Lady Maria.

But she couldn't very well tell Juliana that, nor the rest of the family.

"I should stay for the season," she said. "It is about time I found myself a husband. Another season without one, and I shall truly be on the shelf."

"You know you are the same age as I am," Juliana said with just a hint of a pout. "But I do understand, Emma."

She turned away, her face falling, and Emma felt the guilt wash over her — not because she was choosing finding a husband over spending time with her friend, for Lord knew that would never happen, but at choosing to distance herself from Juliana because of two kisses with Giles.

"Very well," she said with a disguised sigh. "I shall come."

She didn't miss the look on the duke's face this time.

It was one of dismay.

CHAPTER 13

*A*ll in all, it took another day for them to arrange to leave for their country house. Giles would have liked to have departed sooner, knowing that his family was in danger, but his mother would have none of it, saying there was far too much to prepare and that they were already turning what should be a week of preparation into a day.

It was enough time for him to have the conversation with his sister that he would prefer to avoid but he knew was impossible.

He found Juliana in the front drawing room, avoiding their mother. "Are you ready?" he asked, and she nodded.

"I am."

"I need to talk to you about something," he said, and she eyed him warily as she crossed her arms over her chest.

"Go ahead."

"When Emma—Lady Emma and I were looking for you, we came to the house of a woman with whom you are acquainted. A Mrs. Stone in Holborn."

"She *told* you about that?" Juliana came to her feet with a thunderous expression on her face and Giles held up a hand.

"We were both desperate to find you. We went everywhere we thought you could be. It was her last suggestion, and she wasn't pleased that I made her tell me."

"Still—"

"I informed Mrs. Stone that you would not be going there any longer."

"Giles!"

"Juliana, you cannot be traipsing about London in the evening by yourself."

"I'm not by myself. I always take my maid and a footman and—"

"Jules, you are the sister of a duke!" he said in exasperation, uncertain why she didn't understand.

"You sound like Mother," she said, fire in her gaze as she continued to stare at him. "I *will* be going back."

"On this, Juliana, you will not. I forbid it."

"Do you now?" she asked with a raised eyebrow.

Giles nodded. "I do. I am going to speak with the staff and make sure of it."

"Very well, Giles," she said. "If that is how you would like to do this."

"I do," he said, proud of himself for actually being the duke he was and leading them as he was supposed to.

But the pride faded when he saw that look in her eye — one that told him that he was in trouble.

It still bothered him when they departed a day later. The women had packed into the carriage while Giles had ridden beside them, trying not to peer in the window, where he knew he would be able to see Emma sitting with his sister, animatedly chattering away. Juliana had suggested he sit with them due to his injury, but he assured her that he was perfectly fine.

Of course, she had been right — the ride *was* rather jarring — but fortunately it was a short one.

Archibald had stayed in London to oversee the investigation into the previous duke's murder and Juliana's abduction but had sent some of his men with Giles to help protect them through the journey and their stay. Giles had slightly bristled at the suggestion that he could not keep his family safe, but in the end, he knew it was in all of their best interests.

As they were all settling in, he wasn't sure just how he was supposed to address Emma. Did he speak to her as though nothing had happened? Did he take her aside and apologize? That hadn't gone so well the last time he had tried it, but what was he supposed to do?

This was why innocent young ladies were off limits — because most would expect to marry him. Now this one, the one who refused to ever do so — was that what had drawn him to her? — was going to be living in his home.

The day that remained was busy enough that he didn't have to see her until they gathered together, and even at dinner, he allowed his sisters to lead the conversation as he sat awkwardly at the head of the table. It was interesting, that while this was now his home, the family his to direct, he felt like a stranger within it. He had been gone for so long, and over the past year, he had spent most of his time in London where he was usually in Parliament or out at his clubs. The small bit of time they had spent here in the country, he had made sure to always invite additional guests. He just hadn't realized that he had done so in order to not be alone with his family.

The realization was a stark one.

Dinner now finished, the rest of his family had been sitting in various delicate chairs and on the rosewood sofa around the circular table in the blue and gold drawing room while Giles was standing at the window, looking out on the grounds beyond. It was hard to believe it was all his now, even though it had been that way for a year.

"What's on your mind, son?"

He turned to find his grandmother behind him, her blue eyes cutting through him shrewdly. She had always managed to do that — see through all that he had placed in front of him, to what was supposed to remain hidden.

"I suppose I am just considering what a mess this all is, and the fact that I can't seem to do anything about it."

"I wouldn't say that."

"No?"

"You have kept your family safe. You have hired the best you can to determine what happened. I know how difficult it can be sitting around and waiting, but you do what you have to do."

"I suppose you are right."

"What are you going to do about the Whitehall girl?"

"Lady Emma?" he asked, trying to prevent his grand-mother from seeing that she had actually hit upon any truth. "What about her?"

"I am not stupid, son. Do not treat me as though I am."

"I—" he began to deny it again.

"Your feelings for her."

"Feelings?" he said the word as if it were evil. "I have no *feelings* for Lady Emma. She is Juliana's friend. She's like a sister to me."

Even as he said the words, he knew they were wrong, a fact that his grandmother seemed well aware of.

"I cannot say that I have ever seen a man look at his sister in such a way. Do not be a fool, Giles," she said, patting his hand with her wrinkled one. "She's a good girl. One of the few. She can hold a conversation and will never bore you. Be sure to treat her as she deserves."

Giles had no answer as his grandmother walked away from him, but as he stared after her, his gaze travelled to Emma, who sat next to his sister. She must have felt his eyes upon her, for she looked up at him in turn — and even he could not deny the invisible thread that tied them to one another.

What he was going to do about it was another story entirely.

* * *

EMMA COULDN'T SLEEP. Again.

She tossed and turned before she began to pace her room, back and forth, until the walls seemed to be nearing one another, trapping her in the room, despite that it was large enough to house an entire family.

She opened the door a crack and tiptoed out into the corridor. Where she was going, she had no idea. She told herself she was going to the library for something to help her sleep — although whether it was a book or a glass of whiskey, she couldn't have said.

In the back of her mind, however, was the niggling thought that she would be lying to herself if she didn't admit that, deep inside, she was truly hoping that Giles would be awake, that perhaps she would have another midnight encounter with him.

Which was so wrong and made her utterly wanton, but she just couldn't help herself. The man had awakened some-thing within her, something that wouldn't seem to leave her now. Here she had judged him for his rakish ways, and it seemed she was no better than he was.

She didn't know where he slept. She guessed that, like in London, he had left the duke's apartments for the ghost of his father to inhabit, preferring to remain in the chamber that had been his since childhood.

Of course, the chance of encountering the duke — or anyone, for that matter — in an estate of this size in the middle of the night was as unlikely as finding a lost ring in a garden bed.

She padded down the carpeted staircase, her hand on the iron banister until she reached the ground floor. Her footsteps set her on a path to the right and down the hall, and she found herself seeking out the one room in which she always felt the most comfortable — the small drawing room at the back. Unlike the larger, opulent drawing rooms, which were covered in immense portraits of previous dukes and their families, this one was smaller, with pastoral scenes hung upon the soft blue walls.

Emma pushed open the door, finding that the fire was glowing with embers from the day but was nearly extinguished. She placed her candelabra on one of the impressive mahogany side tables and pulled her wrapper tighter around herself before walking to the back windows, lifting the airy, floral-patterned white and blue curtain before placing her fingertips on the edge of the windowsill as she looked out at the grounds before her.

This was the main reason she enjoyed this room. It was the chance to look out on all that the grounds had to offer. Her fingers itched for exploration, and she hoped she would find some time tomorrow to revisit them. The estate offered a trove of vegetation, from the hedgerows to the orangery to the conservatory, where she would have gone now but for the fact it would be rather cool in the middle of the night. The staff that oversaw the grounds was nearly as large as that of most houses alone.

"Somehow I knew it would be you in here."

Emma quickly took in a breath, a tremble running through her entire body at his voice. What were the chances that in a house this size, he would find her, and so quickly? She supposed the chance was not so great if they were both seeking one another out — but was he doing so? Emma wasn't sure if she wanted it to be true or not.

"How would you know?" she asked.

"I've noticed you spend a lot of time in this room," he said simply.

"I enjoy it. It has lovely views, and the blue walls are not quite as intimidating as the red drawing room with all of its gilded edges. In there I feel as though I am in a throne room."

Why was she babbling on? He must think she had gone slightly mad. Emma remained where she was, looking out the window, one hand on the curtain beside her, as she heard him cross the room, his feet padding softly over the carpet.

"Are you following me, Your Grace?" she asked.

"I was in the east library." His voice was so close, just behind her ear, but he didn't touch her.

Another reminder of just how high the man was in society. He had two libraries.

"I thought I heard someone," he continued, his breath brushing against her ear. "You're not exactly stealthy."

"How complimentary. I thought you had more charm than that."

"I do, in most situations. I somehow lose myself when I'm with you."

Emma swallowed hard as he left her for a moment to add a log to the fire and stoke it. She couldn't help but enjoy watching him as he bent slightly over top of it, the fabric of his breeches straining over the hard muscle of his legs. He wore only his linen shirt, which stretched over the breadth of his shoulders as they moved beneath it. Emma had to re-focus herself on what they had been speaking about. She enjoyed a conversation with an exchange of wit, but it had never been like this before, infused with such tension, the very sight of him enough to distract her. She turned her head back to stare out the window.

"I find it hard to believe that a woman as inconsequential as I could cause such a plight."

"You would be surprised," he said dryly, and yet still, he did not touch her, even as Emma twitched, waiting for his warm, heavy hands to settle upon her.

"Planning a tour of the orchards tomorrow?" he asked, changing the subject, laughter lacing his words.

"Actually," she said, holding her head as high as she could, "I am."

"I do hope Smithy allows you entrance. He's quite particular about his gardens."

"As it happens, Smithy and I have an understanding," she said with a fond smile as she pondered the gardener that she had become familiar with over the years. Giles was right — he had been rather perturbed at first that a young noblewoman had an interest in overseeing his work, but when Emma finally made it clear that she only wanted to learn from him, the typically rather crochety elderly gardener became quite amenable to her company.

"Do I have cause to be jealous?"

At that, Emma couldn't help but tilt her head backward to look at him, although she instantly regretted doing so, for he was so close, his eyes so intent upon her that she found herself struggling to breathe for a moment.

"I wasn't aware that you would be jealous of anyone interested in me, Your Grace."

"I believe that's enough of the 'Your Grace' formality, don't you think?"

"I can hardly walk around this palace of a building calling you Giles, now, can I?"

He slowly, gently, lowered his hands until they were resting on her hips, and Emma couldn't help but close her eyes and lean backward into him, causing him to tighten his grip at her acquiesce to his touch.

"Perhaps not in the light of day," he murmured. "But when we are together, alone, I hardly see why not."

Emma anticipated him turning her around to face him, but instead he kept her back pressed against his front, running his hands up and down her sides as she melted into him. His touch was intoxicating, and she understood now what drew so many women to him.

"And just what do you plan on doing with me alone, *Giles*?"

She heard his breath then, hard and irregular, and she realized that he was as affected as she. Was it always like this, then, between a man and a woman? Or was there something different about the two of them?

"It is not what I plan to do with you, luv," he said, dipping his head to nip at her neck, and Emma found herself having to control a moan. "It is what I cannot *prevent* myself from doing."

Emma tilted her head back onto his shoulder, finding it difficult to believe that a powerful duke such as Giles, a man who nearly every woman in London would leave everything for, had any interest in her.

"It's because I'm available, is it not?"

He furrowed his brow. "I am not sure what you mean."

"Your interest in me. There is no other woman available to you for miles, so it is natural that you would be drawn to me."

He stiffened against her back. "Is that truly what you still believe?"

"It only makes sense."

His hands roamed to her shoulders, and he used them to twist her around. Emma started when she saw how intently those blue eyes were focused on her.

"That is the most ludicrous idea I have ever heard, and I will not stand for it."

"Pardon me?" Emma said, her eyes widening.

"I know that we have no true intentions toward one another besides the draw we have here, alone together. I have obligations that you do not wish to be burdened with, and I understand that. However, I must have you know, Emma, that you are one of the best women I have ever known and whoever receives your hand one day will be a very fortunate man indeed."

Emma was still coming to terms with the intensity this charming rake seemed to possess when pushed. Ever since his family had been threatened, a protective edge had emerged, and she had to admit that she enjoyed being under his spell. Even if it was only temporary.

"If I didn't know better, Giles," she said, lifting her head up to his, her lips but a breath away from his mouth, "I would say that you rather like me."

He snorted as one of his hands lifted to caress her cheek.

"In this case," he said moments before he tilted his head down and caught her lips with his, "you are right."

CHAPTER 14

*H*e had kissed her again. Kissed her when he was well aware that nothing would be stopping them tonight except for his own self-restraint.

Which was a frightening thought.

Giles couldn't recall another woman who had been so fiery, so accepting, so giving with herself, and he was having a difficult time remembering that this was Lady Emma Whitehall, the closest friend of his little sister. That she was the child he had once known. For right now, he could only see her as the delectable woman she was.

When he kissed her, she leaned into him with a soft moan that only drew him further to her. She welcomed his tongue, tasting like mint and chocolate and her own particular brand that was the most welcoming and satisfying that he had ever known.

He stroked her mouth rhythmically, reminding him of where else he would like to be discovering her, knowing her, and smiled into her lips when she responded as he had known she would, doing her darndest to become the aggressor herself.

That was not going to happen.

She placed her hands flat against his chest as she lifted her head and stared at him. "Are you sure you are not kissing me because I am the only woman available to you?"

He growled his annoyance. "I am kissing you because I want to kiss you. Because I desire you more than I ever have any other woman. Understand?"

She nodded fervently. "I understand." She breathed quickly as though she couldn't quite catch all the air she needed, and then her hands were warm over the linen of his shirt.

He should grasp her wrists, push her away, send her back to bed.

But she was not a child, and she could put herself to bed when she damn well pleased.

Instead, he caught her hips once more and pulled her tightly against him, spinning her around until she was gripped between the mural of a meadow on the wall behind her and his body on the other side. He lost himself in the kiss, in her, in the way she didn't stop moving beneath him, her hands everywhere, her hips brushing against him in a sinfully agonizing motion, the little purrs in the back of her throat going straight through him until he was as hard as he had ever been against her.

He groaned, knowing that he should let her go, that this was the last place he should be, the last woman he should be with.

"I can feel you thinking," she said against his lips, and he opened his mouth to respond, but then her hands were in his hair, and she was kissing him again.

The line between what he should be doing and what his body was telling him he needed to do was becoming damn blurred, and he blinked as he tried to come up for air and muddle through all that was happening.

"I won't ruin you," he stated, more for his own benefit than hers, and she nodded as she obviously wanted to agree with him but didn't want to say it — a fact he understood.

She pushed against him, and he stumbled backward until the backs of his knees hit the brocade of the sofa behind him. It was a rather dainty piece that he was quite certain he could destroy with his weight, but it was the largest piece of furniture in the room. He sat up, lifting Emma and flipping her down so that she was spread before him on the cushion, and as much as he would have liked to have sat back and taken his time to enjoy what was spread before him, her fingernails were clenched in his shoulders, her legs locked around him, making it impossible.

Giles took one end of the tie of her wrapper and tugged until the garment was open before him, and then rested his hand on her ankle, before slowly working his way upward, waiting for her to tell him to stop.

But instead, her knees fell open as she welcomed him, and he nearly groaned at her perfection. Her skin was warm, silky, and, more than anything — *bare*. He was so close to everything he longed for, and yet it wasn't enough for him.

"I want to see you again," she said, her words just above a whisper, and she didn't need to ask twice. She leaned up to help him with his shirt before she began to run her fingers down over his chest and abdomen reverently.

"Oh, goodness, your wound!" she said when the bandage was revealed. "Are you all right — I'm so sorry, I forgot, I—"

"Emma," he said gruffly. "Stop. I am fine. Trust me, I am no invalid, and I can handle myself just fine."

"Very well. Good. You—you look like one of the statues in the gardens," she said reverently, to which Giles couldn't help but laugh.

"I hope I am slightly more animated than they are."

"Oh, most certainly," she said, before he crouched and

began to lift her skirts even higher, dipping his hands beneath until he could wrap them around her ribs, up higher until he was cupping the swell of her breasts. He closed his eyes and focused on breathing in and out to keep himself under control.

"Oh!" Emma cried, arching her chest up into him, and Giles ensured that he took full advantage this time, his palms running over the soft skin of her breasts, his thumbs tweaking her nipples. Her head dropped backward as she groaned his name aloud, and he would never have imagined how good it would feel to hear it on her lips.

He left her breasts then, this time coming over top of her and unbuttoning the neck of her night rail so that he was able to see one of her breasts, bringing his lips to the center of the first before flicking his tongue against her.

Her lips lifted and at her enthusiasm, he nearly dropped his head and let all go and took her right there.

"Giles... Giles, I—"

"I've got you, luv," he said, taking his time, paying equal attention to her other breast as her nails raked into the tops of his shoulders, and he considered that he could spend all night worshiping her body and it wouldn't be enough. She was too perfect, too ready, too open for him, and he had no idea why it was causing such a mix of emotions to swirl within him.

He had been with women before, and never once had he allowed any into his heart. There was no point, not when he had to spend his life with a duchess who could firmly take control of all of the responsibilities that awaited her.

It was only because he knew Emma so well, he told himself. Why else would he have such a response to her?

He lifted the hem of her nightrail higher and rained kisses over her legs, up her thighs, until she was completely bare to him. She tried to close her knees to him, but he shook his head, nudging them open as he knelt before her.

He could bring her pleasure without ruining her for another. He kissed the inside of one knee again and she jumped at his touch. He continued upward, stroking her thighs, paving the way for his kisses, until he was at the center of her. She stared down at him with wide eyes and an open mouth, until she began to shake her head as though she couldn't fathom what he was about to do.

"No, Giles, you cannot!"

"Can't I?" he said, and then his lips touched her, his tongue tracing her folds. She gasped as she leaned back on her elbows, and when his tongue stroked over her center, she nearly jumped off the sofa. He held her down as he loved her with his mouth, then slid two fingers inside of her. He could feel the tightness of her body before him as she built for him, and then suddenly she was shouting his name as her hips thrust up into him and she tightened around him.

It was so glorious to watch that he nearly spent right there in his breeches.

When he finally lifted his head and met her gaze, her eyes were filled with moisture as she stared at him in shock.

"What was that?"

"That, luv, was real pleasure." He grinned, trying to cover up the tremors that filled him at how doing that for her had affected him. He desperately needed for her to leave now, for he wasn't sure how much longer he could maintain control.

"You should go to bed now," he managed, but she stared at him with so much intrigue he nearly ran away.

"Do you truly want me to?"

"Yes."

No.

"What c-can I do for you?" she asked hesitantly, and he stood and began to walk backward.

115

"Nothing."

"No?" she said, her eyes flicking down to the fall of his breeches, which was currently rather tent-like. "Are you certain?"

He swallowed hard as she stood, her eyes glassy, her lips swollen, her nightrail open at the top. She looked thoroughly debauched and a strange sense of satisfaction stole through him that he had been the one to do it to her.

He stopped when his back hit the wall, and she prowled toward him before sinking to her knees in front of him.

"No, Emma, you cannot—"

"Just as I told you that *you* could not?"

"That was different."

But she was already plucking at the fall of his breeches, obviously entirely unsure of what to do with it, but she was a quick learner and soon enough she had freed him. "What do I do?"

"You do not have to do anything. You—"

But then she had taken him in her hand at the root before she began to slide her palm over him and he shuddered.

She leaned in and tested brushing her lips over the head, causing Giles' hands to fist together as he breathed deeply to try to resist coming right there.

"Emma—" He tried to warn her, but then she was leaning in and wrapping her mouth around his tip. He jerked against her, and then she looked up and met his eyes, surprising him with the pleading within them. Then it hit him — she was asking him for help.

She had no idea what she was doing, and yet she wouldn't stop. Well, that was one thing he could do for her. He slowly, gently, slid in and out of her mouth, letting her get used to the feeling, and her inexperienced yet enthusiastic response left him wanting to place all at her feet, to give her anything she ever wanted. He moved in and out, until he was nearly there, but he didn't want to scare her, knew she likely wouldn't understand what was happening.

He was on the edge when he finally leaned down and placed his hands around the tops of her arms, hauling her to her feet none too gently.

"What are you doing?" she asked, blinking at him. "You didn't—"

"I will later," he said, his voice rough as he rode the very edge of his control. "You need to go."

"Giles," she said, her voice hoarse. "I need more."

"No, you don't," he said, shaking his head desperately. "You need to go to bed."

She looked from one side to the other. "I need *you*."

He knew what she was saying, but he couldn't bring himself to answer her in the manner she desired. "I would ruin you."

"I know."

And then a thought struck him. If he ruined her, he would have to marry her. But would that really be so bad? He had to marry anyway — why not marry a woman whose company he enjoyed? The daughter of an earl would surely be acceptable to his mother, regardless of what she thought of this particular daughter.

And at the end of the day, did it really matter so much what his mother thought? *He* was the duke, after all, and if he wanted to marry Emma, then he would damn well marry Emma.

When he placed an arm beneath her knees and lifted her, he grunted softly as it tugged at his wound, but he glared at her before she could say anything. Fortunately, she let him carry her over to the rug before the fireplace, her eyes lighting with an unexpected thrill as he ranged himself overtop of her, seeking her entrance.

"Are you sure?" he asked her one more time, and when

she nodded, he was filled with a sense of possessiveness that despite all she had said before, she wanted him, wanted this, was choosing him now and for the rest of her life.

He met her gaze as he slowly eased himself into her, but she wasn't having any of that, for she reached up and pulled him down toward her, and he couldn't help himself from sliding into her until she fully surrounded him. He took a breath at the sensations that filled him, different from how it had ever been with any woman before and stopped to give her time to get used to him.

He withdrew, feeling every inch of her, then slid back in before meeting her eyes. "Are you all right?"

"Yes," she said with a hiss, and then wrapped her legs around him and pulled him against her. He was a man lost then as he began to rock into her, back and forth, never breaking contact with the sea green of her eyes, the intimacy striking at something deep within his soul.

She was so beautiful, so enchanting, and he wondered how he had never seen her before. Then she cried out and was coming around him again, and the pulsing finally sent him flying over the edge. He pulled out of her and spent in his hand, over his shirt next to them, until he was empty and sated.

He looked at her lying there, her arms out to the side, her eyes closed, and he wondered if she had fallen asleep.

"Emma?" he questioned, and a smile lit her lips.

"That. Was. Incredible." Then her smile dropped. "Is it like that every time?"

He crawled over toward her, and cradled her head in his hands. "Never," he breathed fiercely. "Never before."

CHAPTER 15

"*W*hy are you looking at me like that?"

Emma had tried to ignore the fact that Juliana had been somewhat distant, but she couldn't any longer. She and Juliana were too good of friends.

"Like what?" Juliana asked, clearing her throat.

"Like you… suspect me of something."

Juliana couldn't know. Could she? Emma supposed a public room of the house was a foolish place to make love, but Juliana was a sound sleeper and not known for roaming the house.

"Very well," Juliana said, edging her shoulders back. "I am not pleased that you told Giles about Mrs. Stone."

"Mrs. Stone? Oh, the animal loving lady?"

"Yes," Juliana said, narrowing her eyes at Emma. "What else did you think I was talking about?"

"Nothing," Emma said quickly — perhaps too quickly. "I am sorry, Jules, I really am. I didn't want to tell him but at the time we needed to find you so desperately that there didn't seem to be any other choice. What did he say?"

"That I am not allowed to go back."

"Will you listen?"

"Of course not," Juliana said, and Emma couldn't help but return the small smile, until both of their lips widened into a grin and they were back to the friends they had always been, united against another — even if it was Giles.

"Where, ah, where is Gi—His Grace today?"

"He said something about reviewing ledgers in our father's study that he had yet to consider," Juliana said. "If you need him for any reason, I'm sure you could find him there."

"I have no cause to need the duke," Emma said, even as heat rose in her cheeks and shot down to her core at the reminder that while she may not *need* him, she most certainly wanted him.

Which was another problem entirely.

She didn't see him again until dinner but did her best to ignore him until his mother began her inquisition of him.

"Are you certain this is the best decision, Giles? How much longer shall we remain here in the country as all of London wonders if we are running from the fact that you did away with your father?"

Everyone around the dinner table stilled at the duchess' words. It had been apparent that she was agitated at being at Remington House just outside Watford when they would typically be in London in the middle of the season, which was most important this year when she had two daughters who were out on the marriage market after their father's death and the following mourning period.

Emma, however, had had other things on her mind.

Most specifically the man sitting at the end of the table, who last night had taken her to a place that she never knew existed. The more she considered it, the more she decided that it was rather criminal that women were labelled all kinds of atrocities for enjoying such a thing while men were able to do so whenever they pleased without consequence. She could hardly see how it was fair, but then, there were many aspects of life that were rather unfair for women, now weren't there?

After making love in front of the salon's fireplace, Emma had remained as long as she had dared before Giles had finally sent her on her way back to her room with a kiss on her forehead and a warning to watch for servants who would soon be up in the early hours to begin preparing for the day.

She hadn't seen him yet today, and when she had tried to surreptitiously ask Juliana where he was, she hadn't missed her friend's sharp look. Emma had tried to laugh it off, telling her that she was merely curious as there were only a few occupants in the house. Juliana hadn't commented any further, although Emma had been able to tell that she had questions.

Throughout dinner, Emma had been having difficulty not staring at him. When he had met her eyes, he had winked, and Emma had bit her lip at the reminder of just what he was capable of.

"So, they think I murdered him," Giles answered his mother now. "What of it? At least we are all safe."

"What of it?" his mother gaped at him. "Giles, do you really think anyone will marry your sisters when our family is embroiled in scandal?"

"Yes," he said simply. "They have a significant dowry, and we are a powerful family. It negates any issue that might surround us."

The duchess snapped her mouth shut at that, while Juliana and Prudence seemed rather uncomfortable. Juliana fidgeted in her seat as if she was trying to decide whether to say anything until she obviously couldn't help herself any longer.

"If a man chooses not to marry me because of potential

scandal, then he is not the man for me," she said, causing her mother's shoulders to shift backward. She opened her mouth, but Lady Winchester spoke first.

"Good on you, girl."

"Mother!" the duchess scolded, but Lady Winchester was long past the point of caring if her daughter admonished her.

"Better to spend your life alone than with a man who would make your life miserable," Lady Winchester continued, pointing her fork at her daughter. "You should know that as well as I, Elizabeth, for you have been far happier since the duke passed."

"Mother!" The duchess was truly agape now. "How can you say such a thing?"

"Because it is true, and I do not believe that your children should have to suffer as you did. Your father insisted that you marry the duke despite my inclinations on the matter. You, at least, have the power to ensure that your children will not have to live such a life."

"I do believe that is up to Giles," the duchess sniffed, and all eyes turned to the lone man, who gave out a bark of laughter.

"Do any of you truly believe that I am the one with power at this table?"

"You are the duke," Prudence said with a shrug, but Giles was already shaking his head.

"We all know that means nothing with the lot of you."

Juliana reached over and patted his hand. "You came through when we needed you to, Giles, and that is most important."

They were all silent for a moment as they were taken back to Juliana's abduction, until Giles finally cleared his throat and looked around at them.

"You may all drive me to drink, but you do know I would do anything for you, do you not?" His sisters nodded. "Even if it means ensuring that you marry men who will, at the very least, respect you as they should."

Emma couldn't help it then — her heart began to escape her chest and lean toward this man who was so insistent on doing what was best for his family. He would do anything for his sisters, it was true. But the question was — would he do the same for his wife? Emma knew better than to suppose that it might be her — nor did she want it to be — but the thought that there was a chance he might do so for another had her falling for him just a little bit more than she should be.

The question was, what was she was going to do about it?

THE NEXT MORNING, Giles found himself awake far earlier than usual and at odds, uncertain of just what he was to do with his time and no other gentlemen in residence.

After a great deal of doing nothing, sitting in his study, unable to concentrate, later in the afternoon he found himself surprisingly headed into the gardens towards the hedgerows. The outdoor staff was just beginning to prepare the grounds for the spring and summer, and while color wasn't flourishing just yet, sprigs of greenery were emerging from the ground, a sign of what was to come if one was patient enough.

He had exited the house through the terrace doors and now leaned his head back as he let the freshness of the country air hit him. He had always enjoyed London as it provided a great deal more entertainment than the country, but there was something to be said about a brief respite to the country. He slid his hands into his pockets as he allowed his feet to crunch over the path that circumnavigated the fountain which was not yet flowing.

His father had been a man of secrets, that was for certain. It wasn't until these past couple of days, however, that Giles realized just how many more secrets there might have been.

"You look like man with much on his mind."

Giles' eyes flew open at the voice, his heartbeat crescendoing and then maintaining its rhythm, although for altogether different reasons when he quickly realized who the voice belonged to.

"Emma."

She was kneeling on the ground, her fingers covered in dirt, a pile of green beside her.

"Please tell me that you are not pulling weeds."

"Very well. I will not tell you."

Giles crouched down beside her. "You do know that I pay an entire team of people a very decent wage to do this for me."

She bit her lip in a way that shot desire he knew very well to his groin and another strange emotion that he hardly recognized to his heart.

"I enjoy it. It helps me think."

"What do you have to think about?"

She looked up at him, her eyes wide and voluminous beneath her long, dark eyelashes. "I think you might have an idea."

With no one around, he reached out and took one of her hands in his, lifting it up and tracing the pad of his thumb over each of her fingers, smiling at the dirt beneath her nails, knowing exactly what his mother would have to say about it.

"What are you doing out here?" she asked. "Are you also pondering us?"

"No," he said, his lips curling up slightly. "I wish I was. Thinking of you is far more preferable to what was on my mind."

She tilted her head as if she could see within his soul, and in a way, he thought she just might be able to.

"Does it have anything to do with your father?" she asked.

"Yes, I suppose it does."

He stood up from his crouch when his thighs began to speak to him, and he held his hand out for her to take. She placed her fingers within his and allowed him to pull her to her feet.

She made no motion to reclaim her hand as they started down the path; nor did he release hers.

"I was here and at your London home so much when he was alive, and yet, I can scarcely recall seeing him," she said, her voice distant in memory. "He was always… elsewhere, I suppose. I never gave much thought as to where that might be."

"It was the same for me and my sisters as children," he said, his eyes not on her but on the horizon, looking out over the manicured grounds and beyond to meadows and eventually the forests that grew of their own accord. He remembered as a boy he spent much time running away and hiding within them, imagining himself being taken in by a pack of wolves and living amongst them like a character from one of his stories. "It was when I left the nursery and was expected to spend more time with my father that I realized how lucky I had been before that point."

"He wasn't a good man."

"No."

"What do you think actually happened to him?"

He looked down at her then, finding her eyes open, curious, but not at all judgemental. Unlike most, she did not believe that he had murdered his own father, and that meant something to him.

"I honestly have no idea," he said with a shake of his head. "I wish I did so that we could put this entire matter to rest.

As much as I hated the man, he didn't deserve to be murdered. I only hope that Archibald can find a clue."

"You did say he is the best."

"He is." Giles paused for a moment. He hadn't meant to tell anyone this next part, but it somehow seemed natural to share it with Emma — even before his own sisters. Perhaps *especially* before his own sisters. "I found something today. Something that I do need to tell Archibald."

"Oh?"

"My father had ledgers out here. Ones that were looked after by the country estate steward. The man has been working out of his cottage and hadn't been to the house until I arrived. I reviewed them today for the first time."

"You found something."

"I did." He drew in a long breath. "Payments. Made monthly to a woman for twenty-five years. They stopped five years ago. I hadn't gone back that far until now."

Emma's grip tightened on his.

"Who was she?"

"She is noted only as Mrs. Lewis."

"Mrs. Lewis? Do you know a Mrs. Lewis?"

Giles shook his head. "I do not. You have never heard of such a woman?"

"Not that I can think of offhand," she said. "I suppose you'd best provide Mr. Archibald with the information and see what he can do with it."

"I suppose you are right," he said as they came to a small gazebo. "Sit with me for a moment?"

She looked back to the house, and he knew what she was thinking.

"No one can see us."

"Very well," she said, the tiniest smile of anticipation dancing on her lips. "Not that you would be planning anything untoward for an innocent young woman."

"Innocent, now, are we?" he asked, wiggling his eyebrows at her, and she couldn't help but laugh.

"I suppose that depends on your definition and comparison."

"Ah, back to reminding me of my rakish ways, are we?"

She dipped her head. "They are rather difficult to forget."

A pang hit Giles in his chest, even as he recognized that he had never been ashamed of his reputation before. He still didn't feel any guilt at how he lived his life — or how he allowed people to consider that he lived his life — but even so, he hated how much Emma judged him for it.

It was on the tip of his tongue to tell her that he wasn't all that she thought he was, but he knew how trite it would sound, as if he was saying so only to placate her.

"Well, then," he said, infusing his voice with the charm that had never failed to sweep a woman off her feet and make her forget all but her own name, "allow me to help you do so."

He wrapped an arm around her back and pulled her up against him as he bent and fused his lips over hers. They fit together as if there was no one else in the world for each of them, and Giles sucked in a breath at how right it felt. Perhaps he *could* do this — commit to one woman and one woman only for the rest of his life. If she was Emma.

Her hands crept up his chest until they were against the base of his neck, and Giles found himself nearly over-whelmed by her once more, until he could practically see her on the floor of this gazebo, her skirts drawn up around her waist as he—

But no. Not here. Not now.

When he finally came up for air, he found that she was breathing as heavily as he was, and he laced his hands around her back as she rested her head in the crook of his neck.

He was a duke. The Duke of Warwick. One of the most

powerful men in the country. And yet he found himself completely unsure of what the next step was. He knew what he was supposed to do — find a woman, court her properly, and then speak to her father.

But instead, he had taken the innocence of a proper young lady and had given them no choice but to marry.

He finally leaned back and placed his index and middle finger under her chin as he lifted her head up to look at him.

"Why haven't you married?"

"Pardon me?" she said, blinking, as if she was having difficulty following the change in subject.

"You have had opportunity to marry. Juliana has told me that your hand has been asked for in the past. Why haven't you agreed?"

She looked down, her eyes focused somewhere on his chest. "I suppose the right man hasn't come along."

"What would make him right?"

"I would love him," she said, lifting her gaze to stare right at him. "And he would love me."

"Do you believe that man is out there?" he asked, holding his breath as he waited for her to answer, hoping against hope that she would say he was sitting right in front of her, that she had changed her mind even though he was a rake, even though he didn't believe in love, she would no longer deny him, as she had said upon their first conversation upon a terrace. It would make everything much easier.

"I certainly hope so," she said her eyes drifting away, over his shoulder now. "I do believe in love, for I have seen it before, in a couple so utterly devoted to one another that they would never consider another."

"Which is why you would never trust me, is that it?"

"I-I never said anything about you," she said.

"You did before," he couldn't help but say, knowing that antagonizing her would help nothing, but deep within him, he was hoping that by pushing her, she would say what he wanted to hear, would tell him that she wasn't as certain in her beliefs about him as she had been in the past.

"I'm sure Lady Maria would understand," she said instead. "She has been raised to turn a blind eye to such discrepancies."

"Lady Maria?" he said, an edge creeping into his words. "What does she have to do with any of this?"

"She is who you are planning on marrying, is she not?"

Anger hovered on the fringe of Giles' emotion. "Is that what you truly think of me? That I would have promised to marry another and then take you to bed?"

He saw her visibly swallow as she stood up, backing slightly away from him. "We never did make it to the bed."

Giles took a breath as he attempted to calm himself. "Emma—"

"I should go. I must prepare for dinner. Juliana will be wondering where I am."

"Emma, we need to talk—"

"Goodbye, Giles."

Before he could say anything else, she was fleeing into the dimming light.

CHAPTER 16

"Well?" Juliana asked as she looked up at Emma from above the needlepoint she was working on. "Do you have something to tell me? Ouch!" She lifted her finger to her mouth, sucking at the blood she had drawn with her needle.

"Why do you continue with the needlepoint?" Emma asked as she frowned at Juliana. "You hate it."

"I do," Juliana said with a shrug. "But it gives my hands something to do when sitting in here for endless hours of boredom."

"We could go outside and work with the gardeners," Emma suggested, to which Juliana arched an eyebrow.

"*You* would enjoy that, yes. However, I would only succeed in ruining my dress and causing freckles to break out across my face, which would lead to lectures from my mother that I have no desire for at this point."

"There is a piece of clothing called a bonnet," Emma said, keeping her tone light. "It serves to cover a woman's face, preventing her from—"

"Oh, Emma," Juliana said with a laugh, tossing a pillow at

her. "Fine. We shall go walk through the gardens, is that a fair compromise?"

"I can live with that," Emma said with a smile as they left the wretched needlework —Emma assumed Juliana's piece was supposed to be a flower, but it was hard to be certain for it could have just as easily been a bowl of fruit — behind as they made their way out of doors via the library. Emma couldn't help but look about for Giles, both disappointed and relieved when he was nowhere in sight.

They stepped into the spring air, a smile forming on Emma's face as they walked through the gardens. She called out a welcome to Sterling and the gardeners, the newer staff seemingly surprised at her greeting while those who had been with the family long enough to recognize her and her interest in their work returned it.

"We are out of doors now," Juliana said, turning to her. "I do not think you can put off sharing with me whatever is on your mind any longer."

"Must I share *everything* with you?"

"You must."

Juliana smiled as she said it, but Emma was aware that her friend would continue to pester her until she told her. She had to come up with something to placate her, for she certainly could not tell her that she had allowed — or begged, she supposed, in actuality — Juliana's brother to ruin her. She could hardly imagine how that conversation would play out.

She hoped that Juliana wouldn't judge her, but she knew how reckless she had been, knew all she had risked for that one bit of pleasure. But it had been worth it.

"It is nothing really," Emma said with a shake of her head. "I have just been wondering as of late whether I will ever truly find love or if I should prepare for a life of spinsterhood."

Juliana eyed her. "You've had three proposals."

"Yes, but finding a husband is much different than finding love. As it is, however, Juliana, I hardly think my marital prospects are of any issue right now when you and your entire family are in danger."

She thought of what Giles had told her, feeling somewhat a traitor for knowing more than Juliana did about her own family. It was not for her to share Giles' dismay, however, and so she kept quiet about it.

"It is so odd," Juliana said, shaking her head. "I was both terrified and yet had a notion that I was going to be fine, that whoever had taken me would never truly hurt me."

"Yet they shot Gi— your brother."

"They did," Juliana said, scrutinizing Emma. "I do think that he was the target. It only makes sense that whoever killed my father was trying to do the same to Giles. Why, I have no idea."

Emma nodded slowly.

"Speaking of my brother…"

A sense of dread filled Emma's stomach as she looked up at her friend.

Juliana cocked an eyebrow. "What is going on between the two of you?"

"Pardon me?"

"I have seen the way you look at one another, how you watch for him when he is not in the room, how he stares at you as though he would like to eat you for dinner. I must admit that it is slightly disconcerting, but I would not *dis*approve of the match. There are certainly positives if you were to end up with him."

"Juliana…" Emma started, and for once found herself at a loss for words. She supposed she should have assumed this conversation was forthcoming, for Juliana was far more perceptive than most realized, but she also hadn't realized just how obvious she and Giles had been. "It is simply a flirtation, nothing more. Likely because I am the only woman in the house to whom he is not related. He has mistresses waiting for him in London as well as potential wives. I do not fall into either category."

Except she had with her actions two nights ago.

"There may be many women lining up for Giles, but I have never seen him so intrigued by a woman as he seems to be with you," Juliana said, looking out into the distance before piercing Emma with her stare. "You are right to guard your heart, however. I love Giles as much as I could love a brother, but he does leave a trail of broken hearts in his wake, and I would most hate for yours to be one of them."

"Of that, I am well aware, Jules. There is no need to worry about me."

"I'm glad to hear it," Juliana said, although she still seemed rather uncertain. "Speaking of the man, there he is."

Emma looked up to see Giles walking toward them.

"We best return to the house," she said.

"I have a better idea. I will return to the house, and you can return with him," Juliana said.

"I would rather walk with you."

"No, you wouldn't. I shall see you back there. I will return to my blasted needlepoint and the hopes that at some point in time we shall be able to leave the dullness of this estate and return to London. Perhaps you might have other… methods to coax Giles into telling you when that might be so."

With a wink, she took off toward the house, leaving Emma to stare after her as Juliana stopped to greet Giles before continuing past him. Emma followed at a much slower pace, until she and Giles met in the middle of the maze of path and hedgerows around them.

"Why did Juliana wink at me and then run away?" he asked, staring after his sister in confusion.

Emma sighed as she stared up at him, losing herself for a moment in the depths of his blue eyes. "Because she has guessed that there is something between the two of us and now considers herself both a matchmaker and protector of my heart."

"Little does she know that her meddling is not required."

Emma looked up at him in surprise and considered him for a moment. She was well aware of what she had done — of what the two of them had done. She was ruined, and if anyone was ever to discover their dalliance, she would hardly be able to show her face in society. Giles would persevere, as he was a duke, although it would be a second strike against him.

But as for Emma... perhaps her opportunity to find love had passed with her one act of passion.

"Why don't you believe in love?" she asked Giles abruptly, and he stopped walking and snapped his mouth shut as his eyes widened.

"Well, I suppose it is too fickle of an emotion. It makes people weak."

"So, you do not believe in marrying for love," she stated rather than questioned.

He looked down at the ground between them for a moment, hands behind his back as he returned her gaze. "I believe that marriage is something of a business arrangement. Partners should be on amiable terms and able to work together. It is best when each brings different strengths into their relationship."

"What if one partner finds someone else to love along the way?"

"That would be most unfortunate. However, I do not believe that would occur, as long as they respect one another.

My parents began their marriage thinking that they loved one another."

"Oh?"

"I should amend that. My mother thought my father loved her. What he actually loved was her dowry. Once he had those funds and had begotten her with an heir — yours truly — he was done with her besides the odd visit to her bed to try to create a spare."

"That is so very sad."

"Yes. It was. They ended up hating one another."

Emma was silent for a moment as she considered what Giles had said and why he thought he didn't believe in love.

Her parents were not exactly a stellar example of a marriage partnership, and yet she had seen what it meant for two people to truly care about one another.

They paused before the stairs leading up to the library's terrace doors. As much as she knew she shouldn't spend too much time alone with Giles, especially where they could be seen, she also did not feel like returning to the house, where she would have to leave his company.

Giles reached out and took her hand in his, gripping it tightly enough that her eyes flew to his face to see what was the matter.

"Do not be frightened of our marriage. I promise I shall do right by you."

Emma's jaw dropped open at his words. "Pardon me?"

His brow rose in bemusement. "You do understand we must marry."

"I do *not* understand that, Your Grace," she said as her heart began to beat faster. What was he on about?

"I may be known as a rake, but I am not the sort of man who would compromise an innocent young woman and then walk away from her. When we were in the salon the other night, I asked if you were sure. I thought you knew what I meant."

"I…" Emma was at a loss for words. She didn't run but found all she could do was stare at him in shock. He was so handsome that it wasn't fair to all the women who looked upon him and couldn't have him, nor to the men who could never live up to all of the expectations he had set for her going forward. But the fact that he had *assumed* they were going to be married… "Do you propose marriage to every woman you make love to?"

"No. I would only propose marriage to a woman like you, an innocent who one would never dally with unless marriage was imminent."

Emma brought a hand to her forehead, finding that a headache was forming. "No."

"Pardon me?"

"No, Giles. I am not going to marry you."

"You have to."

Ire began to cause haziness at the edges of her vision. "I do not *have* to do anything."

"Emma, you could even now be carrying a babe."

"I could, but I likely am not. And if I am, then perhaps we will have to revisit… this. But if we keep this between us…"

"Emma." He stepped closer toward her. "I would never have allowed us to go as far as we did if I had thought you were not amenable to marriage."

"Perhaps that is something we should have discussed prior to what happened."

"There didn't seem to be much opportunity for discussion. I just assumed—"

"Well, that was your first mistake," Emma said, crossing her arms over her chest. "You should never assume."

"But—" He threw up his hands, seeming so desperate that Emma actually felt rather sorry for him.

It was not that she was entirely averse to marrying him. It was just that she had certain reservations about his reasons for wanting it.

"Why did you want to marry me?"

"Why?"

"Yes."

"Well," he ran a hand through his hair, leaving it standing on end as he looked around him as though an answer might appear in the air before him. "We get on well. You already know all there is to know about my family, so there are no secrets there. We are both expected to marry, so why not each other?"

Emma's heart sank at his words. They were practical reasons, and not at all wrong. They just weren't... right.

"Look, Emma," he continued earnestly, "I know you want to marry for love, but is not a friendship with some passion thrown in good enough?"

"No," she said, shaking her head as she stepped around him and started up the stairs. "It is *not* good enough."

He caught up to her just as she was entering the door of the library, and she was about to tell him exactly how she felt when she saw the duchess walk by the doorway. Only, she wasn't alone. Two beautiful women followed her. Women Emma recognized.

"Oh, goodness."

She stopped so abruptly that Giles ran into the back of her, his hands reaching out to catch her before she fell. She nearly leaned back into him, enjoying his closeness once more, but managed to stop herself.

"What's wrong?" he demanded.

"It seems we have company."

CHAPTER 17

*G*iles had wondered what else could possibly go wrong.

He had become the duke, as he had always known he would, and then had promptly been accused of murdering the previous one.

He had finally found a woman whom he was amenable to marrying, had ruined her with the expectation of marrying her, and then found out that she had no interest in a life with him.

Leaving him a bounder without a wife, nor a credible reputation. Then of course there was the fact that his sister had been abducted, there had been an attempt on his life, and he had yet to discover who was responsible.

What was next?

Apparently, being served up the woman his mother expected him to marry.

"Giles, there you are!"

Giles had been taken aback by Emma's sudden change in demeanor, and he had no idea what had caused it. One moment he had been following her into the library, and the next he was running into the back of her before she stormed off into the hall as if he had chased her. When he had followed after her and stepped out into the corridor, he had a sinking feeling as to why she had left so abruptly.

"Mother," he said before looking past her at the women who followed. "Lady Bennington. And Lady Maria. How surprising to see you here."

"How *wonderful*, is it not?" his mother said, turning to eye him with a look that told him not to argue this. "I was so pleased when they accepted my invitation. As we could not return to London for you to continue becoming acquainted, I decided to invite them here."

"Indeed," he said as the butler appeared behind them.

"Your Grace," he said, although Giles wasn't clear whether the man was addressing him or his mother. "Your other guests have arrived."

Giles looked at his mother, brows raised. She might be the hostess, but he was going to have to make her aware that she could not invite anyone she pleased without at least informing him of what to expect.

"Lady Hemingway!" his mother said as the new arrivals walked in. She crossed to the door and air-kissed the woman on the cheek as Giles reached out and shook his cousin's hand. Hemingway took in the scene in front of him and looked at Giles rather sheepishly.

"Not expecting us, were you?" he said in a low voice, and Giles decided the truth here was likely best.

"No," he said, leaning in, "although I must say that I am relieved that there will be another man in the house. I was becoming rather overwhelmed."

Hemingway chuckled as they left the women to greet one another and prepare for the evening ahead. Giles sighed. It was going to be a long night.

* * *

"HE IS NOT GOING to marry her, you know," Juliana said in a low voice in Emma's ear, but Emma simply shot her a look.

"He can if it pleases him," she murmured from where she and Juliana stood in the corner of the drawing room. She supposed it had become something of a house party now, although their numbers were rather off.

"He keeps looking at you," Juliana said in a whisper as Emma tried not to peer in Giles' direction.

"I may have told him something he did not want to hear."

"Which was what?" Juliana stared at her with wide eyes.

"I told him that I would never marry him."

Which was true. She had told him that, the night of the ball at the London house. He obviously hadn't listened very well.

"Whyever not?" Juliana asked, aghast.

"Jules, I know he is your brother, but you know as well as anyone that he is a rake of the worst sort."

"That may be true," she acknowledged, "but he is a love-able rake, and I'm sure he would be faithful to you."

Would he, though? Emma supposed it was a question she had never put to him, although a man could *say* whatever he would like. It was his actions that told a different story.

"I can see that you do not want to speak of this, but I would urge you to consider that Giles is a good man, and, if nothing else, do you not want to be my sister?"

"We already are in every sense, Juliana."

"You know what I mean."

She did. Of course, she would love to be a true sister to Juliana. That would also mean that the duchess would be her mother-in-law, and the woman obviously did not approve of Emma. She could hardly imagine living under the same roof.

She had always pitied whatever woman was to become the future duchess.

"Very well. I can tell that you do not wish to speak of it, but know that I am here for whatever you need," Juliana said before leaning in toward Emma's ear again. "I believe my mother would like me to marry Lord Hemingway."

That got Emma's attention. "How closely are you related to the man?" she asked, crinkling her nose.

"His father was cousin to my father. It could be worse," she said with a shrug. "He is a pleasant sort, but he does seem rather... dull."

"In what regard?"

"He says all the right things, does as he is supposed to, but there is nothing exciting or intriguing about him. He does what pleases his mother, attends events he is expected to, shows up in Parliament when it is time..."

"What else are you looking for?"

Juliana sighed. "I'm not sure. Excitement? Daring? Adventure?"

"Are you looking for a husband or a pirate?"

Instead of laughing, Juliana seemed rather morose at the question. "I'm afraid in this case, I would prefer the latter."

Laughter bubbled out of Emma despite Juliana's plight, but as it did, Lady Maria joined them with a hesitant smile. She was so sweet and beautiful it was difficult not to like her, even though she would likely marry the man Emma had come to know far too intimately. As a matter of fact, she felt both jealous and guilty at the same time as she greeted the woman.

"Lady Maria, it is lovely to see you," Emma forced herself to say as Lady Maria politely noted how beautiful the house and grounds were. They talked about everything and nothing — the weather, the latest in London, the history of the house

— until it was time for dinner, which passed in similar fashion.

The entire evening was one with nothing to note — except the man who wouldn't stop staring at her from across the room, his expression alternating between disappointment, disdain, and disillusionment.

Which was why Emma was actually glad when the knock sounded on her door once all were abed. For she had something to say to the man, and it was best done without an audience.

* * *

GILES HAD WAITED downstairs in the front salon, hoping that Emma would at least come down and have the decency to finish their conversation. He was angry, that he could admit, but he was aware that there was more to it — he was hurt.

Hurt that she didn't want to marry him, yes, but also hurt that she would turn him into a man who would ruin a young woman and then leave her. What did she think was going to happen to her now? Did she really think another would have her?

The very thought of any other man touching her had his hands balling into fists at his sides again, his teeth gritting, and finally he realized that there was only one thing to be done.

He was going to have to go find her.

The first problem was that he wasn't entirely aware of which room she had been given. He couldn't very well ask one of the servants, nor his mother or sisters for that matter.

He did, however, know the wing she had been placed in, for he had watched which way she had walked down the corridor, and he had a suspicion she would be close to Juliana.

Giles had waited in the hall like a stalker in his own home until a lady's maid had left one of the bedrooms, and he distinctly heard her bid goodnight to Lady Emma.

Thank goodness.

He waited until the maid had disappeared around the corner and then walked up and tapped on her door, surprised when it opened seconds later to an Emma who seemed like a toy who had been wound up and was ready to spring open.

"Fancy seeing you here," she said before stepping back and allowing him into the room. Giles looked around him, intrigued at the décor, in cream and shades of purple. It was beautiful and suited Juliana. Interesting that all of this could be his and yet he had never seen any of it before.

"We have a conversation that needs finishing."

"Oh yes, the one in which you are going to convince me to marry you?"

"That would be the one."

"Well, you no longer have to worry, not now that your true betrothed is here."

"Emma, I had no idea she was coming."

Emma had walked across the room and was standing with her back to him in front of the fireplace. Giles longed to cross over and wrap his arms around her, to rest her head back against his shoulder. She, however, seemed determined to keep him at a distance, her anger holding him at bay.

"I know," she said as her shoulders fell and the fight seemed to ebb away from her. "But that doesn't change anything."

"Actually, it does," he said, crossing his arms across his chest and standing as firm as he could, even if she couldn't see him. "I respect my mother but that does not mean that I do everything she asks of me."

"You do what pleases you," she said, her fingers coming to

the mantel as she stared down into the flames. "Have you been to see Maria yet?"

"Been to see—" Giles' anger now was enough to overcome hers and he stormed toward her, taking her by the shoulders and turning her around. "Do you really think so little of me?"

She looked up at him from beneath her lashes, and he could see the regret for her words there, but it seemed she was too stubborn to admit she was wrong.

"You are right. Lady Maria is not the kind of woman who would allow you in, now is she?"

Giles made sure he was gentle as he wrapped his arms around the top of her shoulders, even though he would have much preferred to have gripped her hard and shaken her.

"Listen, Emma, and actually listen for once," he demanded. "I would never even try to see Lady Maria in such a light because she does not interest me. Not in the way you do. I do not find myself looking around, trying to determine if and when she is going to walk into a room. I do not wait with bated breath, wondering what the next word out of her mouth will be. I do not watch her as she eats her meals, laughs with the other women, or walks about the room because I am wondering just what it would be like if all her attention was on me. There is only one woman who causes such feeling in me, and I think you know that woman is you."

CHAPTER 18

*E*mma sucked in a breath, frozen by the intensity of Giles' stare, the force of his words. Surely he couldn't mean—

"I thought you said that you wanted to marry me because it was convenient."

"That is not what I said."

"It is what you insinuated."

He ran a hand through his hair, and it was so endearing that Emma nearly broke.

"What are you trying to say?"

"That I want you with a passion the likes of which I have never wanted another. That ever since we were together, I can think of nothing but doing it again. Tell me that you don't feel the same."

She opened her mouth to deny it but closed it again, unable to say anything to the contrary. What he said was true, but could a marriage be based upon such an explosive passion that was bound to eventually flicker down to nothing?

"I do want you," she mumbled. "That I cannot deny."

"But?" He waited.

"But I am not sure that we can build a life upon that. Tell me this, Giles. Did you always plan to be true to your wife?"

He broke contact with her gaze then, looking to either side of her head. She could tell he wanted to say yes, and looked so strong, so masculine standing there that Emma was tempted to forget all the tension between them and show him how much she did want him.

But that would only prove him correct.

"I never really thought too much about it," he admitted. "Before you, I suppose I *intended* to be honorable to my wife, but I doubted that I would actually be able to do so."

"My husband must be true to me," Emma said firmly as she dug her nails into her palms at the thought of Giles with another woman.

"Of course, I would be true to *you*," he said so passionately that she nearly believed him.

"You have changed, then?"

"I have, actually," he said, but his voice lacked the conviction she needed.

Giles with another woman had started a string of thoughts in her head that she couldn't quite force out.

"How many women have you…bedded before?"

He pushed away from her shoulders as he turned around and walked a few paces away from her. "None of them matter."

"But they do — to me."

"Emma," he turned around, his blue eyes glinting hard, although with an intensity for what she wasn't entirely sure. "The women before you… they were part of a mutual understanding that we were both getting something that we wanted out of the arrangement. There was no meaning behind it. We didn't know one another. Not like you and I know one another."

"So, the fact that we knew one another prior makes a difference?"

"Yes!" he exclaimed, his hair now standing on end from the amount that he was running his hands through it. "I never would have gone so far with you without assuming marriage was on the other side."

Emma was aware that he was not a man who'd likely had many such conversations. She supposed he could use a good deal of practice on sharing his feelings with a woman.

She swallowed hard. She knew what was missing. It was love. What she had been wanting in a marriage from the start. She supposed there was a chance it could grow, but if it wasn't there already with the friendship and passion they seemed to share, she couldn't imagine where it would come from.

"I—"

"Did you hear that?" he said, cocking his head.

Emma sighed. To what lengths would he go to in order to halt such a conversation? "Hear what?"

"It sounds like… there are footsteps downstairs. Which is odd. Everyone should be abed, and it is not yet early enough for any of the servants to be awake."

"Perhaps there are other assignations going on tonight," she said, cocking one of her brows, to which he shot her a look.

"The only other man here is Hemingway."

Emma shrugged, doing so only in order to tease Giles, and it seemed to be working as he obviously finally determined just who Lord Hemingway would be interested in.

"I'm jesting, Giles," she said, taking pity on him, as she heard a thump as well — which must have been quite loud for it to have reverberated all the way here to this wing.

A hard knock sounded on the door and Giles and Emma looked at one another in panic.

147

"You cannot be found in here!" she hissed at him, and for a moment she thought he agreed, but then a wicked gleam lit his eyes as the corners of his lips turned up while he stared at her.

"Or what if I am?" he murmured.

"Giles," she said, lifting a finger in the air as she took a step toward him. "I will not be trapped into marriage. Not like this."

He paused for another moment, before looking around him with a shake of his head.

"You would never know that I own all of this," he muttered before he dove to the other side of the bed as the knock sounded again.

Emma rushed over to the door and opened it a crack, but Juliana didn't seem to take the hint and pushed by her into the room, shaking her hands in front of her in agitation.

"Oh, good, you're awake."

"Yes, I—"

"There is something going on downstairs. There was a crash and I heard running, and then a shout. I was going to go check but I thought perhaps going alone wasn't the best of decisions."

Emma heard a low muttering from the other side of the bed, and when Juliana instinctively began to turn her head toward the sound, Emma walked toward the doorway so that Juliana would have to follow her.

"Very well. Let's go check."

A slight scuffle that neither of them could ignore sounded across the room and then Emma looped her arm through Juliana's and forcefully turned her toward the door.

"What was that?" Juliana asked, and Emma shook her head.

"Nothing. Come, let us go see what is happening downstairs—"

"Not alone."

"Giles!" Juliana exclaimed, her mouth dropping open as she turned from her brother to Emma, who could only stand there and show her displeasure by placing her hands on her hips and silently fuming at the man. "What are you doing in Emma's—oh."

Her mouth stayed rounded in its O as she stared at one of them and then the other, as Emma shook her head.

"We were simply having a discussion."

Juliana nodded slowly, although it was obvious that she didn't believe her.

"I needed to explain to her that I had nothing to do with Lady Maria's arrival," Giles said, and that did seem to slightly help matters as Juliana's mouth shut at last. "Emma didn't give me a chance to speak with her today, so I saw no other option."

"I see. Well, this is all very… intriguing."

"Indeed," Giles said dryly. "But there are obviously more pressing matters to attend to at the moment. The two of you stay here. I am going to go see what is happening."

He walked out the door and Juliana stared at Emma with so many questions in her eyes that Emma nearly had to laugh.

"I promise I will tell you more, but in the meantime, can we please follow him and see what is happening?"

"Of course," Juliana said, taking her elbow, and Emma was reminded once more why they had always been the closest of friends.

They kept Giles in their sights as they crept after him, pausing at the top of the stairwell until they began to make their way down. They were halfway down when they heard the butler addressing Giles.

"Oh, Your Grace. Thank goodness."

"Taylor! What is amiss?"

Juliana and Emma exchanged a look at the state of the butler, who was currently also dressed in a robe over his night clothes.

"It seems someone has been in your chambers. We heard the crashing from above, and your valet and one of the footmen went to check that nothing was awry. They saw a figure emerge from your room in a hurry and make his way out of the house. They tried to follow him but lost him in the dark."

Giles placed his hand on the rail, and while they couldn't see his face, the white of his knuckles showed how affected he was.

"No one saw him? How did someone enter the premises without anyone noticing?"

"I'm not certain, Your Grace."

"Where are the men who are here to apparently protect us?"

"They were surveying the grounds, which is what they are doing now. They are trying to determine how someone entered the house and found your chamber."

"Damn it," Giles cursed. "Thank you, Taylor. Return to your bed. We will determine what to do about all of this tomorrow."

"Are you certain, Your Grace? Rogers is currently reviewing all the items in your room to ensure that nothing was taken."

"Yes, I will go speak to him. Thank you."

After Taylor walked away, they heard Giles sigh. He didn't turn around when he said, "You two might as well come down here."

Juliana and Emma exchanged a look before they padded down the staircase. Giles looked anything but the usual jovial, carefree charmer of a rake he typically was. Instead, it seemed as though he was bowing to the weight of responsibility that had overtaken him.

"I suppose this is what it truly means to be a duke."

"What do you mean by that?" Juliana asked, but Emma knew. For so long he had tried to be someone completely opposite to the man his father was, someone his father would disdain, and in the process, he had lost himself. Now he was trying to reconcile the part he had played with the role he had no choice to take on. And he had no idea what had happened to the true Giles.

He continued as though he hadn't heard his sister. "All I want to do is keep all of you safe. But it seems that trouble follows us at every turn."

"That is not your fault."

"No," he said, his gaze faraway. "But I do not seem to help matters." He finally focused on the two of them. "Both of you should be back in your chambers."

"What are you going to do?" Emma asked. "I don't think you should return to your room. If someone was there after you, what is to stop them from returning?"

"Why, Lady Emma, are you offering an invitation?" Giles asked, a twinkle in his eye for a moment as he studied her, and Emma's cheeks warmed in response as she stole a glance at Juliana, who was back to gaping at the two of them.

"No!" she exclaimed. "I am simply concerned for your safety."

"Well, I am equally charmed by that," he said. "Not to worry. I will sleep somewhere else."

"Very well," she murmured, suddenly wishing she was anywhere but here. "Giles — how did he know you weren't in the duke's quarters?"

His lips pressed into a firm line. "I do not know, but I would suppose that someone within must be providing information. One of the servants perhaps. But we will reconvene in the morning," he said. "We will all have much to speak about."

"I still have a great many questions," Juliana chimed in, and Giles rolled his eyes at his sister.

"I am sure you do. But there is nothing to say."

"Do you love Emma?"

"Juliana!" Giles and Emma exclaimed at the same time, and Emma found that she couldn't look anywhere in Giles' direction. She was too worried about what she would see on his face if she did. Likely a man who was ready to run as far from her as possible at the mention of the word.

Juliana, for her part, was smiling smugly. "I see I have struck a chord. On that note, goodnight."

"Goodnight, Juliana," Giles said, before reaching out and grasping Emma's fingers. She looked up at him with wide eyes, even as heat travelled up from where they were joined to spread throughout her body. "Goodnight, Emma," he said.

His words were like a caress. As something else, something she couldn't name, blossomed in her chest, Emma could do nothing but turn and run up the stairs as if she was being chased, Juliana following behind her.

CHAPTER 19

*G*iles leaned his head back against the headboard behind him. He was in a strange room that had hastily been opened, one he didn't even recognize. While it had been aired in case it needed to be utilized, it still smelled musty and the fire hadn't been lit long enough to properly warm the room.

Taylor had briefly suggested the duke's chambers, but Giles had dismissed the idea before Taylor could even finish the thought.

He knew at some point in time he would need to take over the duke's living quarters, but not until all remnants of his father had been removed. He hardly needed to be surrounded by the man's possessions.

So here he was, wide awake in an unknown chamber in the wing of the estate that also happened to house the bedrooms of his sisters and Emma.

Emma.

As soon as he had heard that there was danger on the property, all he could think of was how fortunate it was that he had been with her — not for his own safety, but that it meant she was fine. He couldn't help himself from thinking of the nights she had been wandering the property alone. What could have happened to her if someone else had been there, waiting for him but finding her instead? He ran a hand over his face as he tried to push the imaginings away, for they were more than he could bear.

Dear Lord, what was happening to him? The woman had taken over his thoughts, both during sleep and the day. This had never happened to him before. He had always been the man to find his pleasure and leave.

A fact which Emma herself seemed awfully perturbed by.

Giles still intended to marry her, but he was beginning to realize that perhaps he would have to wait, at least until all of this danger was behind them. The problem was, however, that perhaps the most danger to her was from him. He could barely keep his hands off her.

He thought of what she said, of needing love to make a marriage work. If only she could understand that love was fleeting. It could end as quickly as it began. It was not the foundation of marriage.

Although neither, he supposed, was a passing fling. He was still rather chagrined that he hadn't been able to keep himself in control, to hold himself back from her. Now that she had refused him, he found that he wanted nothing and no one but her.

It was a damned conundrum. Sometimes he wished he could just pick up and leave all of this behind — the rules, the responsibilities, the dukedom itself.

It wasn't a new thought. He had considered running away a time or two before.

Only now he couldn't imagine running away alone.

* * *

"WE ARE GOING to return to London."

His mother stared at him in shock.

"But Giles," she began, "we cannot return to London. Our guests have just arrived."

He had convened his family — and Emma — in the drawing room. He had come to a decision in the early hours of the morning, a decision that he knew they were not going to like but was necessary.

It was time he finally started to think about what was best for his family, which was not always necessarily what they wanted.

"I know," he said, "and we will take a couple of days to prepare ourselves to return. I have written Archibald and asked him to have everything in place in London by the time we arrive."

"Have what in place?" his mother asked.

"All that we will require to keep our family safe," he said. "I thought that coming to the country would protect us, but obviously I was wrong. For now, I would like everyone moved to the same wing of the house and we will have the few of Archibald's men who are here guard that wing. However, I believe it will be best for us to be in London. Then we will not have additional guests to deal with, and the London house is much smaller for the same number of men to better ensure our safety. I will also be able to help Archibald determine who is threatening us."

"Do you have any ideas who that could be?" Prudence asked, and Giles swallowed as he thought of his father's ledger. He had sent Archibald the information, but he preferred to visit this woman for himself to determine who she was and what hold she'd had over the previous duke.

"Not as of yet," he said, ignoring Emma's look.

"I shall have to tell our guests," his mother said dejectedly, but before Giles could respond, his grandmother did for him.

"It was foolish of you to invite them in the first place, Elizabeth. Now *you* shall have to deal with it. I taught you better than that."

"Mother," the duchess began, her eyes closing for a moment as she took a breath to control herself, but her mother waved away her words before she even began.

"We need to learn to deal with consequences. Isn't that right, Giles?" she looked up at him with such knowing that he wondered if she had somehow guessed what had happened with Emma, which was ridiculous, unless his grandmother had some ability to read his mind. It was a scary thought, but if there was ever a woman who could manage it, it would be Lady Winchester.

"Er— yes," he said. "If you could please speak to the staff, Mother, we should be prepared to leave in two days' time."

"Very well," she said, rising with a dramatic sigh and as they began to leave the room, he wanted to stop Emma. He wasn't sure why, there was something within him that needed her touch, needed her to tell him that all would be well, that he was doing the right thing.

Which was ridiculous. He was the duke, and seven years older than she, at that. He knew better than anyone what needed to be done.

So instead, he watched her go along with the rest of them.

But why did it hurt so much that she didn't even turn to look at him as she left?

* * *

After Giles' announcement that morning, Emma found that she needed some time to think, so she did what she always did — she went to the place where she could find some peace.

She would have preferred being outdoors, but she chose

to actually heed Giles' warnings and stay within the house. One could spend weeks on the property and never discover all it held, as it was.

The orangery was beautiful, of course. It held some of the most exotic plants, the likes of which she hadn't seen anywhere else. She wondered whether anyone in the family even realized the treasures that were held within. She could hardly believe the expense of their upkeep, but then, that was not exactly a worry for them, now, was it?

She walked over to the Bougainvillea trailing over a post, picking off a few leaves that were turning yellow, capturing them in her hand.

"Doing my gardening again, are you?"

She turned quickly to the entrance to find Giles leaning against it. He was so undeniably handsome, yet he also looked so tired. Emma found that her pulse began to quicken when she saw him and took a few steps toward him until she was standing an arm's length away.

"You're making the right decision," she said, somehow knowing that he needed to hear her say it.

"It's hard to know sometimes," he said, looking past her shoulder at the room behind her, although Emma guessed that he wasn't actually seeing any of it.

"What are you so concerned about?"

One corner of his lips quirked upward, but there was no humor in his half-smile.

"What am I not concerned about?"

"You are looking after your family. That is all anyone can ask of you."

"I should have stayed and learned more about what it meant to be a duke. Instead, I let my hatred of my father overwhelm all, and I—"

He couldn't seem to say anymore, and Emma tilted her

head as she looked up at him. "But you have said that he is not the man you wanted to be."

"No."

"So be your own man. Don't worry about what your father would or wouldn't have done. Do what *you* know is right. As for the rest of it — well, you have stewards, solicitors, and a man of business to help you with that, do you not?"

"I do. But—"

"You do not need to take everything on your own shoulders," she said, before standing on her tiptoes and reaching out to him, smoothing away the wrinkle line that was indented into his forehead. He let her do so before reaching out and catching her hand, then used it to pull her in until she was flush against him.

He reached out and wrapped his arms around her, tucking her head beneath his chin. He tightened his grasp and just held her there for a moment, so close that Emma could actually feel tension easing out of him.

"Thank you."

"For what?"

"For being here. For being you."

"Of course," she said with a small laugh.

"Emma," he said, his voice even more serious now, and she stiffened slightly. "I'm sorry."

"For what?"

"For not… for not controlling myself around you. What I did was unforgiveable, but I must tell you that I had full intentions of marrying you, that I never would have compromised you if I didn't think you were agreeing to marriage."

She stepped back slightly and looked up at him. "We've discussed this enough. No more apologies. I was a willing participant."

"Emma—" He looked pained, which hurt her in turn.

"I promise you," she said, "I enjoyed every minute of it."

To silence his protests, she placed her lips on his, which had the desired effect. He lost control as quickly as he ever had, his lips slanting over hers, and it took but a few moments until he was the aggressor, pulling her in as he assaulted her mouth, and she could only sigh into his as she lost herself in the kiss.

She had no idea what the future held for her, or for them together, but she did know that she was going to enjoy this moment and all that he had to offer. He might be a rake, but if anything good had come out of that, it was the talents he had picked up along the way — those, she was not going to complain about.

When he finally eased away, Emma found herself disappointed — but what did she think, that he was going to take her again here in the orangery amongst the plants? Although that did have a certain appeal, she had a feeling that he wouldn't be making what he felt was a mistake with her again.

"What happens now?" she asked. "When we return to London?"

"You will return to your family, and I will determine who is threatening mine," he said, bemusement on his face as to why she would ask.

Which made sense. She had told him that she didn't want to marry him. So why was she so upset that he was finally listening?

"Of course," she said, nodding.

"Emma," he caught her hands between his. "I meant what I said. I will marry you."

"Because you are obligated to."

"It's not only that. I have told you—"

"Yes." She stopped him. "We are friends, and we have passion."

"You know I am there for you, no matter what."

"I do," she said before standing on her toes and placing a kiss on his cheek. "Goodbye, Giles."

She meant for the moment, of course — she would be seeing him again at dinner.

But as she walked away, it was with the knowledge that there was much more to that goodbye.

And it broke her heart.

CHAPTER 20

*T*hey remained in the house together for the next two days, but they might as well have been on opposite sides of the country. Emma hardly spoke to him, and Giles had a feeling he knew why. There was so much emotion tying them together that it was only going to make the parting that was bound to happen seem that much more difficult.

What frustrated him was that it didn't have to be that way.

But upon her refusal, Giles had let her go. He had given all he had to give, had made his offer. He could only hope that she would eventually see the sense in what he had suggested.

In the meantime, his mother was using their last two days in the country to their full potential. She made sure that Lady Maria was available to speak to him at every turn, was sitting next to him at every meal. Giles also noticed that she similarly tried to pair Juliana and Lord Hemingway, although the man hadn't seemed to realize it yet, while Juliana seemed rather ambivalent at the implication.

It cheered him slightly to know he wasn't the only one in his mother's sights.

He had heard back from Archibald as well. The detective had tracked down the woman, Mrs. Lewis, but had yet to draw a connection between her and the previous duke. As Giles had requested, Archibald would wait until his return to make any contact with her.

Giles had also ensured that he was now sleeping in the bedchamber next to Emma's. He might not be able to go to her — for that would only tempt him further — but he would stay as close as he could to ensure her safety. It was the least he could do.

Then it was finally time to return to London. The convoy of carriages prepared, Giles mounted his horse to ride beside them, noting that his wound no longer tugged at him when he did so.

"Mind if I join you?"

Giles looked to the side to see Hemingway trotting toward him, and he shook his head. "Of course not. It would be nice to have the company."

"I couldn't take another trip alone with my mother in the carriage. Not that I don't love her and all, but—"

Giles chuckled. "I have enough females in my family to understand that sentiment."

They started back out, the wheels churning and horses' hooves knocking on the ground.

"Speaking of females... my mother discussed something with me last night that was rather eye-opening."

"Oh?"

"It seems that she and your mother have a plan of sorts."

Giles lifted a brow. "I would assume that this has some-thing to do with Juliana?"

"You assume correctly," Hemingway said, eyes wide in

surprise. "I had no idea. I suppose I should have and feel rather daft now, but—"

"Not to worry, chap. It is the way of things."

"Right." Hemingway was silent for a moment before he finally began speaking again. "Now that my mother has spoken to me about it, I suppose, well—if Lady Juliana isn't opposed, perhaps I could speak to her again once we return to London?"

Giles was so surprised he twisted in his seat to look at the man. "Are you asking my permission to court her?"

"Well, I—I suppose I am."

Hemingway looked nearly green, and Giles had to laugh.

"I have nothing against the thought of it," he said. "However, as you will come to know if you don't already, Juliana is her own woman, and I cannot tell her to do anything she wouldn't like to do. If she would like to be courted by you, then by all means, go ahead, but if she declines the offer, then I cannot do anything about it. Understood?"

"Understood," Hemingway said, blowing out a breath as some of the tension seemed to melt off him after their discussion. "Now, about this threat to the family — what can I do to help?"

* * *

THE CARRIAGE RIDE SEEMED INTERMINABLE.

Emma caught sight of Giles out the window now and again, but the divide between them seemed greater than ever before.

Juliana seemed to understand that Emma didn't feel like talking about what was bothering her — or perhaps it was simply that her mother was in the carriage and she knew that nothing could be discussed in front of her.

But she didn't press, not even when they stopped for a mid-afternoon break, and for that, Emma was grateful.

For what was she supposed to say? That she was falling for Juliana's brother, a man who had compromised her and vowed to marry her, a fact she should be celebrating? No one would understand that she couldn't marry a man who didn't love her — nor one who would likely leave her bed for others once they were married.

A rake was always labelled such forbidden fruit — a man who would be the best lover, the best kisser, who knew how to please a woman.

But what if you were the woman he was promised to for the rest of his life? What did it mean to be attached to such a man?

It would mean heartbreak, and ruin.

Emma had never wanted to be the woman who reformed a rake. She had wanted to be the woman who resisted one.

Yet look where she was.

Giles would likely marry a woman like Lady Maria. One who had learned well enough to turn her head when he left her bed, who would do as was expected of her without a word of complaint.

That was one thing Emma would never do. Even if, despite her best of intentions, she ended up married to a man who didn't love her, he at least best respect her. She would not be the woman all of London gossiped about who couldn't do enough to keep her husband happy.

It was hard not being able to talk to Juliana about it all. She was the one who always understood, who supported Emma indisputably. But Emma could hardly explain all she was feeling when it was Juliana's brother at the center of her concerns. Juliana would see him in a different light and wouldn't be able to separate her love for him from Emma's best interests.

When they returned to London, the carriage stopped at Emma's family's home. It was far less grand than the duke's London mansion, of course, but the townhouse on the corner of Berkely Square was quite respectable.

Emma bid her farewells to the family, telling them she would see them soon, and then started up to the house.

She looked back at Giles, so handsome and regal on his roan horse, sitting next to Lord Hemingway.

She longed to run toward him, to thank him and attempt to say enough that would repair everything between them, but she had no words, nor any opportunity.

Instead, she simply nodded her head and then stepped inside the house.

* * *

GILES WASTED no time in contacting Archibald. The detective arrived by noon the next day.

"Thank you for coming so quickly," Giles said, leading him into the study, reminding himself that he still hadn't done anything to erase his father's ghost from the room.

"Of course," Archibald said, taking a seat. "All has been quiet for the most part. No one has been near the house. I did hear you had some excitement in the country."

"Which is why we are back," Giles said, tenting his fingertips and leaning forward. "It seems that I cannot keep my family safe no matter where we are."

"We should have sent more men," Archibald said, the turn of his head and set of his jaw the only signs that he wasn't pleased with himself. "I didn't think your troubles would follow you to the country."

"Well, it seems we were both wrong," Giles said. "We were still too close to London, I expect. Should have escaped to

Scotland, but we cannot run forever. All we can do is get to the bottom of this as quickly as we can."

"When would you like to visit the woman from your father's ledgers?"

"This Mrs. Lewis? Have you discovered anything about her?"

"She lives alone. She moved to London not long ago, from a village near your family's estate."

"Somehow I cannot believe that is a coincidence."

"I doubt it."

"Does she have family?"

"I heard rumor of a son but have not heard any more of him."

"Interesting."

"I had a man watching her house but have returned him to Warwick House now that you are here. I have all available resources watching over your family."

"Good," Giles said. "I think it is best just to knock on the woman's door. Not to give her a chance to run."

"I agree."

"We go tomorrow," Giles decided. "If you arrive at three, we can leave from here."

"Very well."

They both stood and walked to the door, just in time to see a swish of skirts enter the drawing room, and Giles' heart started to beat faster as he realized just who else had arrived. They had left everything with so much uncertainty that he knew he would have to talk to Emma once more, to decide once and for all if there was anything between them.

He just hated how much it scared him to do so.

* * *

HE CAUGHT her when she left the house, following her until she had rounded the corner past the front gates so that Juliana wouldn't be aware that he was speaking with her.

"Emma."

She started, one hand coming to her chest when she swiveled around quickly to find him there. He walked toward her, sparing her maid a quick glance.

Fortunately, the mansion was back far enough from the road that no one would see him take her arm alone.

"Do you have time for a walk, perhaps back through the gardens?"

She seemed hesitant as she shifted her weight from one foot to the other until she finally nodded. "Very well." She looked to her maid. "Lydia, would you follow us back and then take a seat on one of the benches where I am in sight?"

The maid nodded dutifully and then followed along behind. Giles waited until she had taken her seat and they were out of her hearing before he began.

"I'm sorry for how we left things."

"As am I."

He walked her into the maze. The hedgerows were only waist-high, leaving the rest of the gardens still in view.

"I've thought a lot about it. Us. Marriage."

"Oh, yes? Have you come to a conclusion without consulting me?" She stopped and looked at him, her face inscrutable before she continued. "Let me ask you something first," she said, her head dipping down before she lifted it to look into his face. "Do you love me?"

Giles felt a clawing panic in his chest as his throat seemed to close. He had never wanted to love. It was too treacherous, made a man too weak, allowed him the ability to be destroyed. Besides that, it was fickle, uncertain, something he had always vowed to avoid at all costs.

The thought that he could be in love — it terrified him.

"I—" He tried to say the words, but they wouldn't seem to come. For the truth was, he had never felt the same way about another woman as he did about Emma. She was everything to him and he could hardly imagine life without her. But love? He didn't even know what it meant to love, or why it mattered so much to her.

"Your silence is answer enough," she said, her eyes glistening for a moment, breaking his heart.

"Emma—"

"I asked. And you told me. That is better than a lie."

"I do want to marry you." And he did. That was the truth, as much as it scared him that he *could* fall in love with her. He would just have to make sure it didn't happen.

"I will not marry a man who doesn't love me," she said, shaking her head, looking away, off into the distance. "I've thought a lot about it, and I think—I think you should marry Lady Maria. Or a woman like her."

Giles hadn't known that anything could frighten him more than the thought of being in love. But the thought that Emma might leave him, that she didn't want him? That caused a panic that made it difficult for him to breathe.

"You want me to be with another woman?"

A flash of pain crossed her face.

"Would you not be with other women regardless?"

"No," he said swiftly, and he realized that it was true. "I would never go to another woman. Not if I was with you."

"They are lovely words but an easy promise to make."

"You think so little of me." The words were out before he realized it, bitter as they were released from his mouth. "You believe yourself so pure, making it so easy for you to judge me and my past."

"I am not judging you," she said sharply. "You have always been free to follow your desires. It irks me beyond measure that as a man you can do as you please without society

168

thinking any ill of you, but one rash act and I will be forever ruined."

"Is that what you would call what happened between us? A rash act?"

"It *was* rash, was it not? Neither of us was thinking."

"But I *was*," he said fiercely. "I had decided at that point that I would marry you."

"Well, then," she said, straightening her shoulders. "I am so glad that you came to that decision. However, you forgot to consult with me."

"I assumed—"

"We talked about assuming," she said, and then with a big sigh, the fight seemed to go out of her. "I'm sorry, Giles," she said, her voice just above a whisper. "It is what it is. We are not meant to be together. Not like this."

She took a step backward, and then another. "Goodbye," she said, and then turned toward her maid.

Giles wanted to run after her but found himself frozen in shock, unable to believe what was transpiring. He had always been under the assumption that he could have any woman he wished, but now the only one he wanted was walking away from him, without a clear explanation as to why. It wasn't his fault he couldn't love her. He had told her that from the start.

"Emma," he called out, unable to help himself. "What about you?"

She turned around and looked at him. "What about me?"

"Do you — do you love me?"

Why had he asked? What difference could it possibly make? Yet somehow her answer meant everything to him.

She paused, staring at him for what felt like hours but was likely only a few moments.

"Yes."

And then she was gone.

CHAPTER 21

"*I* thought I'd find you out here."

Emma rose so quickly that a muscle in her back twinged, and she cursed herself for being so easily startled.

She was normally much more observant, but she had been too lost in her own thoughts.

"Juliana," she greeted her friend, before the entire situation came rushing back and she looked around quickly. "Should you be here? I thought you were confined to the house."

"I'm not alone," Juliana said as she meandered the narrow walking path toward where Emma was digging in the small garden plot. It wasn't much, but her parents had allowed her to look after the small bit of land behind their London house while they were in residence. "Giles has ensured that I am well guarded. There are two men following me, as well as my maid."

She gestured behind her, to where the two men stood like sentries on each of the entrances into the small garden area. Abigail sat on a bench near the front of the garden.

"I'm glad to hear it. Have they made any progress in determining who is threatening your family?"

"No," Juliana said with a sigh as she took a seat beside Emma on the second bench. She tugged at the strings of her bonnet, pulling it off her head and setting it beside her as she looked up at the sun.

"Your mother is going to be greatly put out if your freckles emerge."

"I know," Juliana said with a laugh. "But I don't overly care. Besides, how can *you* say such a thing when you spend all day out here?"

"I have my bonnet on."

"Still."

They were silent for a moment, enjoying the light conversation between them, reminiscent of the time before everything became so much more difficult. Before Juliana's abduction, before the constant danger, before Emma fell in love with Giles and her heart shattered into pieces.

"Are you going to tell me what happened?" Juliana asked, as in tune with Emma's moods as she had ever been.

"What do you mean?"

Juliana eyed her. "Do not play the fool, Emma."

Emma sighed and placed her spade back into the dirt. She was just beginning the plantings for the spring and summer. She would have to leave it to the gardeners when she returned to the country, a thought that was already causing her great remorse as she realized she would have to go with her parents and not with Juliana, for it would now be far too difficult to spend the summer in the country with Giles.

"Very well," she said, taking a seat on the bench beside Juliana. She played with the skirt of the old dress she had worn for gardening before deciding that it was best to simply be blunt. "I am in love with Giles."

Emma wasn't sure what she was expecting from Juliana

— shock, outrage, surprise if nothing else. But Juliana simply smiled and said, "I know. So, what is the problem?"

Emma sat up and looked at her. "Why aren't you surprised?"

Juliana rolled her eyes. "Emma. I know you better than I know anyone else in the world, likely even Prudence. I think I should be able to tell when you have fallen in love — particularly with my brother. He obviously feels the same way about you, so why are you here, wallowing in the garden?"

"I am not wallowing."

"You are. Usually, you are much more joyful when you are here. You look as if you are digging a grave instead of a place to plant your beloved flowers."

Emma eyed Juliana. "Very well. I was wallowing."

"Why?"

"Because!" Emma exclaimed, her hands rising in front of her, sending pieces of dirt flying. "Despite what you say, he does *not* love me back."

"Of course he does."

"He does not," Emma shook her head. "Trust me. I asked."

"I see," Juliana said, biting her lip. "That must have been difficult to hear."

"It was." Emma willed the anger to build up within her in order to push away the pain and sorrow that threatened to rise.

"Well, Giles is just being an idiot," Juliana said decidedly. "He doesn't know what he wants."

"Jules," Emma said softly. "He is your brother, which is why I didn't say anything to you earlier. It puts you in quite a difficult position. Trust me, I would have preferred to have fallen for anyone *but* him."

"Why?" Juliana said, a slight defensiveness in her tone. "Giles is a good man."

"He is, of course he is," Emma said. "But he is your *brother*, meaning that it will be difficult for me to now spend as much time in your homes as I once did. And then there is the fact that he… well, he…" How did one note to a man's sister that her brother was a rake? "He enjoys the attention of many women. I cannot see him being true to only me — especially if he does not love me."

Juliana was silent for a moment, and Emma wondered if she had said too much.

But then Juliana rose, determination on her face, and Emma realized that she *had* said too much — but not for the reasons she had thought. No, she had given Juliana a mission, which was a scary thought.

"Jules, please do not do anything."

"I won't," Juliana said, but her hand was behind her back and her face belied her words.

"Just because you are crossing your fingers does not mean that you can lie to me," Emma said with a slight roll of her eyes.

"Emma!"

"You were the one who noted that we know one another far too well, and I am aware of what you do when you are lying," Emma said, standing with her. "Please do not say anything to Giles. It is what it is, and I will get over it."

Only, Emma was the one lying now. For one thing was for certain — she would never get over Giles.

* * *

GILES STOOD on the doorstep with Archibald beside him, wondering just what he was going to find on the other side.

At least he knew that nothing could further shatter the memory of his father. For he had learned long ago just what type of man his father truly was.

There was a pause after he knocked, and then the door

173

slowly opened. It was dark within, and Giles could barely make out the woman inside.

"Good afternoon," he said with a nod, trying to seem non-threatening. "Is this the home of Mrs. Lewis?"

There was a pause, and the door remained nearly shut but for a crack.

"Who is asking?"

Archibald stepped forward, as he and Giles had discussed the fact that the woman likely wouldn't welcome the Duke of Warwick at her door if she had known the previous duke.

"My name is Matthew Archibald, and I am here on a delicate matter, if we might come in?"

"I'm not sure that is wise."

She made to close the door, but Giles reached out a hand to keep the crack from closing. He didn't push her further, but he didn't want to lose this one connection that might help his family.

"Mrs. Lewis, I promise we are not bringing trouble."

"You can say what you have come to say from out there."

The woman obviously had reason to be scared, which bothered Giles. What could his father have possibly done to her?

"Very well," Giles said, looking at Archibald who nodded back at him. If his father had been paying her, perhaps she could be enticed by the promise of more payments.

"I am the new Duke of Warwick. I know my father was paying you and I have come to see if I owe you anything further."

There was a pause behind the door, and then a slight sigh.

"No. I want nothing more from your family."

"Mrs. Lewis, may I ask what the connection was between you and my father?"

"No."

"But—"

Before he could say anything more, she shut the door in his face. Giles stood there with his mouth agape before he looked over at Archibald, who was grinning at him.

"Never had a door slammed in your face before, have you?"

Giles closed his mouth. "No. I do not suppose I have."

Archibald shrugged. "You get used to it."

He started down the stairs.

"Where are you going?" Giles called after him.

"We're not going to get anything else from her by pressing her. We'll find out the information we need another way."

"How?"

"That's what you're paying me for, is it not?"

Giles stomped down the steps after him rather moodily. "You haven't done much so far."

To his surprise, Archibald nodded. "You're right. I haven't." He paused. "We do have a lead, however, regarding the threat to your family. I didn't want to tell you until I was certain, but we think we know who took Juliana."

"You do?" Giles heartbeat quickened.

"We do. We were able to get some descriptions of the man and tracked him down. A so-called friend of his told us most of what we needed to know for a rather paltry payment. Now we just need to find him."

"The sooner the better," Giles muttered, wanting to get past all of this and move on with his life, whatever that meant. He thought of Lady Maria and the future that awaited him and nearly cursed aloud.

"You will be the first to know when we make our move," Archibald said as they mounted their horses and headed back toward Mayfair.

Today had been another day that brought little fruit.

It seemed to be an ongoing theme in Giles' life.

* * *

WHEN HE RETURNED to his study, Giles had full intentions of reviewing more ledgers from years past to see if he could unearth anymore of his father's secrets. But as he stood there looking around the room, he decided he'd had enough.

He walked over to the wall that faced his desk and stared up at the portrait that looked down at him with judgement.

"I think we've had just about enough of that," he said, before lifting it from the wall and placing it on the floor.

He walked over to the window and tugged at the heavy curtains. He couldn't seem to move them back, so instead he pushed a chair over, stood atop it, and lifted the entire rod out of its moorings. The room was instantly flooded with light, and Giles smiled with grim satisfaction. He began to determine his next course of action when there was a knock at the door.

Some hopeful part of him wondered for a moment if it was Emma, but he instantly pushed the thought away. Of course it wasn't her. She had no reason to be here — he had made quite sure of that.

"Come in," he said, surprised when his grandmother walked in. She said nothing at first, but looked around the room, her eyes eventually settling on him.

"Good. I'm glad to see you are finally ridding us of his presence."

"Grandmother," he said in surprise, although he really shouldn't be shocked, as she always said exactly what she was thinking.

She snorted. "You know how much I disdained the man," she said, walking into the room, her cane thumping against the floor until she reached the thick carpet. "He was horrible to this entire family, but most especially to you."

"He was. But then I left the rest of you to face him alone when I ran away."

She studied him for a moment. "You did not run away, Giles. You were chased."

He had no quick response for that, so instead swept out a hand. "Sit, please. Is there anything you need?"

"Yes," she said, gracefully taking a seat, her hands on the head of her cane as she looked up at him. "I need you to get your head out of your ass."

Giles blinked. "P-pardon me?"

"The girl you let walk out of your life. You best go get her back while she still loves you."

He sank into the chair across from her. "It was her choice. I offered to marry her."

He hadn't thought he would ever share that with anyone. Not after Emma had turned him down.

"I am assuming you did something to necessitate marriage?" His grandmother arched an eyebrow and heat flooded Giles' face.

"Most ladies do not speak of such matters," he mumbled, to which she laughed.

"You know that I am not 'most ladies.'"

"That you certainly are not."

"And your Lady Emma is also not 'most ladies.'"

"No," Giles said as an image, unbidden, of Emma rose to his mind. "She is her own woman entirely."

"I am going to assume that you made some grand speech about how she has no choice but to marry you."

"I did, but what is wrong with that?"

"Did you tell her how you feel about her?"

Giles looked down at his hands, feeling like a young boy who was being chastised. "I did."

"And she still didn't stay?" He had finally shocked his grandmother.

"I told her I didn't love her."

She lifted her cane and smacked him on the side of his arm. "What the hell is wrong with you?"

"Grandmother!" His mouth hung open in shock at both her language and her action as he rubbed his arm.

"Oh, come now, I know I am not saying anything you haven't heard before."

"Not from my grandmother!"

"Why would you tell her that you don't love her?"

"I do not."

"Do you not?" she said, tilting her head. "Why do you think that?"

"I—" He opened his mouth to respond, but nothing came out. He had always told himself that he couldn't love, that he wouldn't love. And then Emma had walked into his life. He thought about her nearly every moment of the day, and — quite obviously — had difficulty keeping his hands off her. But when she had asked, he had panicked, not wanting to admit to her — or to himself — just how he truly felt. "I was scared," he finally finished in a small voice.

His grandmother nodded in satisfaction. "Of course you were."

"Of course?"

"It is terrifying to fall in love." She smiled wistfully. "I should know."

"You loved Grandfather?"

"I did. Very much," she said. "I could never bring myself to remarry, despite him passing so young."

"Did either of you ever… fall out of love?" He couldn't help but ask, curious now, and she shook her head slowly.

"Never. Our love was true. Pure."

"My parents—" he began, unsure how to put his thoughts into words.

"They did not love one another," she said swiftly, shaking

her head. "They were infatuated with one another for a brief period of time. There is a world of difference."

Giles interlaced his fingers and leaned forward. "How do you know?"

His grandmother smiled at him. "There is no right answer to that. It is different for everyone. But I suppose one could say that you must consider whether you crave this person to be with you for a moment, or whether you need her by your side for a lifetime?"

The answer stuck in Giles throat. For at that moment — he *knew*.

He was in love with Lady Emma Whitehall.

His grandmother stood and smiled triumphantly.

"Now the question is — are you going to face your fear and do something about it?"

CHAPTER 22

$\mathcal{G}$iles stepped into the door of the club — Aphrodite's it was called. It was not one he had ever entered before, not here in a rather seedy part of London, but it was where Archibald had told him to meet.

He hadn't made it far when the detective was at his side.

"Not to worry," Archibald said in his ear. "I know the owner. We're safe here."

"I wasn't worried," Giles countered, although there was a part of him that wondered if it was the best of ideas for him to be here, especially when there seemed to be a target on his back. He felt mildly better when Archibald pointed out his men stationed around the room.

"The man we're after is at the back," Archibald said, pointing to a table surrounded by about ten men. "We're going to wait until a few of his friends disappear. It could be a while, so you might as well get a drink and enjoy yourself."

Giles nodded and found himself at a small table where his back was to the wall and he could see the entire club before him. A barmaid approached his table, a sparkle in her eye. She was rather buxom, her bodice low, and with the curl of her black hair over her shoulder, she was exactly the kind of woman who had always tempted him.

Earlier he had wondered if perhaps this would be the answer to rid Emma from his mind — to find another woman to offer him some pleasure, erase the mark she had left upon his soul.

But as the barmaid sidled up to his table, her blue eyes gleaming at him, he found that nothing within him stirred — not even his usual libido.

"Can I get you anything?" she asked, leaning in, making it obvious that it was not just a drink on offering.

"An ale," he said, although he found that he didn't have much appetite for drink either.

"Very well," she said, pushing back before placing a hand on the back of his chair. She leaned down and whispered in his ear, "if there will be anything else, just look for me. I'm Lydia."

"Thank you, Lydia, but just the ale will be fine," he said firmly, and she nodded, disappointment in her glance as she walked away with a swish of her hips.

Giles stared after her, thinking of his grandmother's words.

He loved Emma. He knew he did. For the thought of life without her? It was bleak, boring, one that he wasn't sure he could face.

He was still terrified that she might fall out of love with him one day, decide that she was better off without him.

But as for him? He knew now, without a doubt, that there would never be another. Not now, not ever. Being with her had given him a taste of what a life of love could be like, and he never wanted to lose that.

Now he just had to convince her of how he truly felt.

He found himself rising from his chair to go do exactly that — although how, he had no idea, in addition to the fact it was after midnight — when a faint whistle caught his attention, and he turned to see Archibald nodding to the table, where just three men remained.

It seemed there was other business to attend to first.

By the time he reached the table, Archibald had cleared away the other men, leaving only one behind, who was looking around as though in search of a saviour. But there were none to be found here tonight.

"I don't want no trouble," the man was saying, holding up his hands, and Archibald took the seat across from him, leaning back with his arms crossed over his chest, his hat low over his eyes.

"There doesn't have to be," he said, "if you tell us what we need to know."

"Of course," the man said, and only then did Giles see that another man was now sitting next to him, one he recognized as one of Archibald's — and he had a pistol pressed against the suspect's side.

"Do you know this man?" Archibald nodded at Giles.

The man nodded as sweat broke out on his brow. "The Duke of Warwick."

"Correct. Your Grace, this is Cillian Reynolds. Reynolds, why don't you tell us how you know the duke and his family?"

"I—I don't know them myself. I was hired, though."

"To do what?"

"To take the girl. Hold her hostage."

"And then?"

"And... and then shoot the duke when he came to get her."

Giles felt rage begin to grow from deep in his belly that this man had threatened to harm his sister, his family, but he knew that to stand up and punch the man in the face wasn't going to help anything at the moment.

"Who hired you?"

"I don' know."

"Reynolds." Archibald shifted forward into the man's face. "This can go one of two ways. You can tell us what we need to know of your own will, or we can *make* you tell us what we need to know."

Giles looked at Archibald with some new respect. He hadn't known that the man had it in him.

"I promise you that I am telling the truth," Reynolds said, his hands up in front of him. "I'll tell you how it went. I'll tell you everything. I was here, in the bar, when I got a note. To meet a man in the back alley. He had business for me. It was a good sum of money, so I went out back. Took a friend with me, if you want to ask him. It was too dark to see the man's face, but I heard his voice. He told me what he needed, gave me money then and promised double the amount once the job was finished. So I did what he said. Took the girl, then went to the place the man had told me to take her. I was to leave at a certain time and then return. Figured he wanted a look at the girl. I wasn't to touch her, wasn't to do anything to her, but wait for the duke and not let her go. So that's what I did."

"And then I arrived," Giles growled, trying to keep himself in check. "Were you supposed to kill me?"

Reynolds nodded vigorously. "The bit—the girl yelled out for you. Somehow got out of her gag. I fired a shot, but must have missed you and then there were men everywhere and I figured it was best to run. Couldn't get my money if I was dead."

Giles didn't want to give Reynolds the satisfaction of knowing that he had hit his mark.

"You know nothing else about the man who hired you?" Archibald pressed, but the man was vigorously shaking his head.

"Nothing. He didn't contact me again. Never got my

money. S'pose it was because I didn't kill you." He looked at Giles without any regret, and then Giles couldn't stop himself and did what he had been itching to do.

He stood up, cocked back his fist, and punched the man in the face. He shook out his arm as he looked at Archibald.

"Get whatever else you can from him and then take him in to the magistrate. I'm going home."

With that he stalked out of the club, rage and frustration simmering within him.

And he knew that through all of this, there was only one thing, one person who could make him feel any better.

Emma.

* * *

EMMA MET Juliana the next day in the early afternoon at the front doors of the museum. Juliana had a particular love of Roman antiquities and had asked Emma if she'd like to visit today, to bring her some peace, she said, as she was feeling rather on edge.

Emma hadn't particularly felt like leaving her house or her garden, preferring to "wallow" as Juliana had put it, but she knew her friend had been through quite a bit over the past while and therefore couldn't bring herself to say no.

"It makes sense," Emma said after Juliana arrived and they began climbing the stairs. "You've had much to be concerned about lately."

"I wish I wouldn't let it get to me," Juliana said. "I waited all morning for Giles to learn what happened last night as he was going to see Archibald. Not that he told me he was going, but I found a piece of correspondence informing him of the meeting. I was nearly tempted to follow him, but we all know how he's reacted to that in the past."

Emma couldn't help but laugh at that as they continued

up the stairs to the museum. They had just reached the entrance when a young boy tugged on Juliana's dress.

"'Scuse me, miss?" he looked to Juliana.

"Yes?"

"This is for you."

He held a piece of paper out to her, which she took and read quickly, her eyes widening. She passed it to Emma wordlessly.

You escaped the first time, but best watch yourself. Your family is not fit to hold its title, and we will be coming for you. In time, all of your secrets will be revealed.

Enjoy the museum.

"Oh, Juliana," Emma said, bringing her hand to her mouth. "We best go home."

"What should we do with it?"

"I suppose we shall have to tell Giles."

"Do you truly think so? He hasn't been quite himself the past while, and this is only going to make it all the worse."

"You have to tell him, Jules. How could you not?"

Juliana nodded morosely as they made their way down the steps. One of Archibald's men was beside them in a moment, his hand out for the note. Juliana and Emma exchanged a look before Juliana shrugged and passed it to him. His jaw tightened and he asked them to get in the carriage, as both men tightened around them and their maids.

The thought of Giles had Emma's stomach churning, but she couldn't very well not accompany Juliana home over her fear of seeing him.

It would be the first of many times to come, she told herself. Like it or not, she was just going to have to get used to it.

CHAPTER 23

"What in the…?"

Emma and Juliana walked through the front door of Warwick House only to find staff busy walking to and fro, while Juliana's mother seemed near to apoplexy.

"Mother?" Juliana said as she looked from one side to the other. "What is going on?"

Her mother stopped when she spotted them in the entrance, then she turned to them and placed her hands on her hips.

"Juliana. There you are."

"What is amiss?"

"Your brother."

"What about my brother?" Juliana asked, even as Emma's heart started to beat faster as she immediately wondered if something had happened to him.

"He woke up this morning with some inane ideas in his head. He's out back in the gardens, clearing a space in the middle of the grounds, heaven only knows why, but he already has the builders here and…"

She continued to speak, but Emma had tuned her out as

Lady Winchester approached. "I would say it is for you, my dear."

"For me?" Emma's eyes widened, as Juliana turned to her with a grin while the duchess stopped talking mid-sentence.

"I told you he loved you," Juliana said smugly, but Emma was shaking her head.

"I don't understand."

"I don't suppose you will until you go outside and see what all the fuss is about," Lady Winchester said, tapping her cane on the ground with authority.

"Go," Juliana prodded her. "I'll walk you as far as the terrace."

"But Juliana," Emma protested as Juliana practically pushed her along the corridor. "What about the note?"

"It can wait."

"Are you sure? I really don't think—"

"Emma!" Juliana said in exasperation. "Giles is not a man who goes to a great deal of effort for anything. You might as well see what this is all about."

"It's not necessarily for me. We are assuming—"

They had reached the terrace, however, and Juliana pushed her outside the door. Emma turned around to tell her that she should at least come with her, but Juliana had locked the door behind her.

"Juliana!" Emma exclaimed as she banged on the door, but Juliana just grinned at her and waved toward the grounds. Emma sighed as she turned around, facing the inevitable.

Her eyes immediately widened.

Giles had certainly been hard at work in the short time Juliana had been gone. The grounds were filled with a team of men, who were clearing an area right in the middle of the green. It was the site where she had previously remarked that a garden bed should be added, that would be the perfect place to grow the rose garden of her dreams.

What was he doing?

A path ran from the terrace straight to the center, and Emma folded her hands over each other at her waist as she took slow steps down the path toward it. She felt as though she was walking down the aisle of her wedding as she placed one foot in front of the other, nearing the building. What if this had nothing to do with her? What if she was only going to make a fool of herself by listening to Juliana and Lady Winchester? She would be far better to — *no, Emma, you can do this* — she told herself, taking a deep breath.

And that's when she saw him.

He stood in front of the cleared space, his shoulders broad and strong, highlighted by the sun streaming behind him. She knew the moment he caught sight of her, when his head turned toward her and he stilled.

Emma waited for him to tell her to go, to wave her away, but when he didn't she found she could do nothing but continue toward him. She tried to remind herself of all the reasons she should be running from him, that she had asked him to leave her be.

And found that she couldn't remember a single one of them.

For all she could think about was him. Giles. The man she loved with all her heart, the man she wanted in her arms, in her bed, in her life.

She tried to keep her steps slow, steady, even. But as she neared, they quickened, and then he began striding toward her, until they were nearly running to one another, and Emma cursed the size of the green that it would keep them apart for so long.

When they finally met, Emma longed to push herself off the ground and throw herself into his arms, but instead she stopped a foot from him and he followed suit, watching and mimicking her every move.

"Emma," he said, her name on his lips in a pant, and she returned, "Giles," even as she found she could barely form a word for her heart was beating so hard and not from her run from the house.

"I'm sorry," she started, needing to reach out to him but knowing she had to say this first. "I judged you for your past, I made assumptions, and I—"

"Emma," he said, stepping forward, reaching his hands out now, slipping off her gloves and taking her bare hands in his palms. "I appreciate that. I do. But I must say something first."

She nodded slowly, parting her lips as she waited, wondering what he could have to say, what he was doing, what could possibly have changed, if anything at all.

"I was a fool," he began, and when she opened her mouth to contradict him, he placed one finger against her lips. "I was. I was a fool because I allowed my fear to overcome all else. I was scared, Emma. Scared of loving you, scared of what could happen if I did, of how broken my heart could be if you ever denied me or walked away from me. But then you left anyway, not because I loved you, but because I told you I didn't. And you know something?"

He looked at her now with a rueful smile. "It hurt just as much as it would have if I had told you I loved you. Because the truth is, Emma, I *do* love you. I love you more than I ever thought possible, more than *seems* possible. I know because I cannot imagine my life without you. The thought that you might rather be without me… it makes me feel… hollow. But if that's what you want, I will respect it."

Emma swallowed, looking past him at the greenery beyond. "What is all this?"

"This? This is for you."

"But what is it?"

"I'm having them clear a space to build you a flower bed, a

foundation to breed the roses as you've always wanted. I don't know anything about them or if this is even the right climate for what you want, but if we need to build an enclosure around it, then we will."

Emma could only stand there in shocked silence before she finally said, "You were fairly certain this would work."

Giles laughed, although there was nervousness in his chuckle. "I certainly hoped that it would help convince you. But if you don't want me—" his voice broke in a rather endearing way, "—it is still yours. You can come visit Juliana and do what you wish with it."

"Oh, Giles," she said, her voice hoarse as she looked at him. "Do you truly believe that I could possibly live without you?"

"I—I don't know."

One moment, Emma was frozen, trying to take in all that he said and all that was before her. Then in the next instant she thawed, and all of the emotion came rushing through, the joy that he felt this way, the relief that she wouldn't have to go through life not knowing his love, the indescribable swell of her heart that this man wanted her — and not just for one night, not just because she was the only option available to him, but because he saw a life with her.

She took a step closer, until the toes of her boots were right against his. Slowly, she raised her arms until they were wrapped around his neck.

"Giles," she said, her voice just above a breathy whisper, "I love you too."

The grin that broke out on his face was warmer than the sun on a mid-July day.

"Will you marry me, then?"

"I will," she said, forgetting all else as his lips came down on hers and she let herself bask in the glory of his love, of what it felt like to be cherished by this man. Everyone else wanted him because he was the young, handsome Duke of Warwick. She wanted him because he was Giles. Her Giles.

He lifted his lips from hers, resting his forehead against hers. "I want to grow a family with you, just as you can grow your gardens, here and in the country. It's all yours."

"What do you suppose your mother is going to say about all of this? Oh, and Lady Maria. Oh, dear."

Giles gazed down at her with a glint in his blue eyes. "I don't give a fig about what my mother might say. I am the Duke of Warwick, and it is time that I start acting like it. I am the one who will spend the rest of my life with my wife. Not my mother. And as for Lady Maria, well, I am sure she will find someone more suitable. Someone who could perhaps give her love as well. Love that I would have been unable to provide her. Not like I will you."

He leaned down and whispered in her ear. "I don't suppose you would walk with me around the grounds?"

Emma shivered as his breath on the most sensitive part of her neck sent a tremble through her. "I would go anywhere with you."

"I am glad to hear it," he said, as they passed the workmen and headed into the trees.

Emma curled her fingers around his arm.

"Giles, I know I have always been rather… judgemental of your reputation as a rake, and I wanted to apologize. I should never have held your past against you, and it seems that there are a few advantages to being with a man who is rather experienced."

She stole a glance at Giles, who actually seemed somewhat contemplative at her words.

"There is something I should tell you."

"Yes?"

"I am not as much of a rake as you believe me to be."

Emma stopped walking. "What does that mean?"

"It means... that while I deserve some of the title, I am not nearly as... prolific as I had people believe. I cultivated the reputation, encouraged the rumors, to spite my father. I never realized that I would one day come to regret doing so."

"Interesting," Emma murmured. "While I do enjoy knowing the complete truth about you, I must say that I no longer care about your past whatsoever. Either way — you are yourself and you are now mine, and that is what matters."

He squeezed her hand. "I am glad to hear it."

"Do you suppose anyone can see us from the house?" Emma asked as they meandered around the hedgerow, and she knew immediately where they were going — to the small gazebo that overlooked the edge of the river that ran along in front of it. It was quite secluded and offered protection from both the elements and prying eyes.

"I most certainly hope not," he said as he led her into the small structure, placing her down on the bench, "but if they do, then it is at their own folly. I've already ruined you once, have I not?"

He knelt in front of her, and Emma leaned down and took his face between her hands. "Let's not call it ruined, shall we? I do despise that word."

"Very well. What shall it be then? Deflowered?"

"No!"

"Spoiled?"

"If only to spoil me for others."

"Ravished?"

"That works."

Then his lips were on hers again, but this time it was not just a slow promise of love, but also a promise of all that could accompany it.

CHAPTER 24

*G*iles knew that he should wait, that he would have this woman for the rest of his life, but at her yes, at her declaration of love, at her promise of forever, he found that he was filled with every sensation that was so quintessentially Emma. Her scent floating around him, her curves beneath him, the peppermint chocolate on her tongue — it was just too much for him to resist.

The gazebo might be an ill-advised idea, but he would be rational, he promised himself.

And then he started kissing her and promptly forgot everything else. Which was exactly what had led to their previous trouble, but then that trouble had led to forever, so really, what did it matter?

"You have too much clothing on," he murmured, "but I suppose I am just going to have to work around it."

"A challenge for you, Your Grace?"

"One that I am willing to face for you, love," he promised as he reached up and tugged at her bodice, releasing her breasts, admiring the view in front of his face. If it was possible to get even harder than he was, it happened at that moment as he reached out and cupped them from the bottom, leaning in and tasting the tip of first one breast and then the other. Emma moaned out a breathy sigh from above him, and Giles found himself overcome by how lucky he was to find a woman so responsive, so eager for his touch.

Her hips lifted toward him as he continued to suck, his hands molding her breasts as he didn't stop lavishing her with his tongue, enjoying it just as much as she did. He was leaning up toward her, and she reached down to try to find him. When he was too far away, she settled for moving her hands over his shoulders, down his sides, and he was overcome by the fact that she also couldn't seem to get enough of him in turn.

"Giles," she groaned out, "this is sweet torture."

He grinned as he rocked back on his heels away from her, his hands coming to the hem of her dress. She looked down at him with wide, glassy eyes and rosy lips, causing Giles to wonder if he had ever seen anything so delectable before in his life.

He lifted her hem slowly, raising one of her legs and trailing kisses up to her knee, kissing the underside before continuing up, until her skirt was around her waist and his lips were inches from her.

"Oh, Giles," she said as he placed a kiss right in the very center of her, before leaning in and taking the bud of her in his mouth. She gasped and nearly arched up off the bench, but he was there, holding her, and she finally relaxed into it, placing her hands on the bench behind her to hold herself up as she bared herself to him.

"What are you doing to me?" she asked as his tongue swirled over her, giving her all the pleasure he could as his fingers inched up her legs until they were on her sex, and he found her opening and slowly stretched her. She bucked against him, needing more, which he gave, promising himself that he would never keep anything from her again, that he would return everything she offered him as many times over as he could.

His other hand came up and played with first one nipple and then the next, until she was nearly melting off the bench into him, her breath coming faster, her eyes closed shut and her jaw tight. Then in one spellbinding moment, she was pulsing around him, capturing his fingers, and when it finally ebbed, Giles sat back away from her, pleased with himself and taking great pleasure in the sight of her fully ravished before him.

"That was…." She trailed off, apparently unable to properly put into words her opinion on his ministrations.

"Good," he said with a satisfied grin. "I'm glad."

He stood up and reached out to straighten her skirts, but she placed a hand on his. "What are you doing?"

"I am attempting to return you to some semblance of order."

"But we are not done."

"Are we not?"

She reached out a hand, trailing her fingers up the tent in his breeches. "I do not believe so."

"Emma, we can't—"

"I want more," she bit out, her words just above a whisper, and he tried to say no, tried to tell her that this wasn't the time or place, but found that he couldn't properly form the words.

With inexperienced yet unhesitant fingers, she began to unfasten the fall of his breeches and he leaned in, letting her continue. "I cannot seem to deny you."

"I shall remember that."

He managed a gutted smile.

"My body will always be yours — and yours alone — to do with what you will." She looked up at him then, her eyes meeting his, the connection between them so strong that he felt it deep within him.

A determination grew within her, and he knew then what she wanted in this moment — she wanted to be in charge, to be the one to lead the way. And he was happy to allow it.

She drew him closer, using him against her in tight strokes, and he leaned over her, his hands on each side of her hips.

Giles reached out and lifted her then, turning her on the bench so that he could straddle her and the seat and find where he needed to be.

"Emma." He said her name again as the desire for her shocked him with its intensity. He lined himself up at her entrance, looking up at her with question in his eyes, and she nodded her head with such absolute assurance that he knew without question she was the one for him and always would be. He sank into her, and her head tilted backward as she allowed him in, but her eyes remained open, on him, until she was stretched around him. Giles reached out, took her hips, and with a thrust seated himself fully within her. He lifted her so that her bottom was on his thighs, and he took a breath to maintain his control as she relaxed around him.

When he felt she was ready, he lifted her up, then brought her back down on top of him. Gently at first, although it was near *too* gently, and she leaned in and took his earlobe between her teeth.

"Again," she demanded, and he reached out to lift her again, only this time she moved with him, thrusting herself down upon him harder now. He let her move with him a few times until he began to lose his control, needing to show her exactly how much he wanted her and only her. He lifted her up in the air and began to pump his hips up and into her, taking greedily as he slapped against her while she moaned into him. He tugged at one of her nipples with his mouth once more, nearly coming in the moment.

Except he needed more.

"Emma, do you trust me?"

"Yes," she breathed, and he lifted her up off him and turned her around, placing her hands on the bench and her feet on the floor.

"Tell me if you want me to stop."

"Don't stop."

He bent her over and came up behind her, easing into her again, groaning as he did so. "Still all right?"

"Yes, Giles!"

He heard the impatience in her tone and would have laughed if he wasn't so gutted by her acceptance of what he wanted, of the ease in which she gave herself to him. He tried to wait a moment for her to settle around him, but then she was moving against him and he knew that he wouldn't be able to wait any longer. Nor, it seemed, did she want him to.

He gripped her round bottom, squeezing before running his hands up around her hips, as he pulled himself all the way out and then forward again.

"I love you," he said as he rocked into her. It became a chant as he moved against her over and over, thrusting in, showing her what he felt as he told her. She was his, and he was never letting her go. Then she was pulsing around him again and sending him over the edge, going still as he came into her, filling her, branding her, making her his.

When he was finished, he lifted her off of him and pulled her to him, kissing her again, murmuring his love for her in her ear, and she returned all he gave until he knew they had to go inside or he was liable to take her again.

"We best begin planning that wedding for as soon as we are able," he murmured.

"Three weeks?"

"You forget who you are marrying," he said with a grin. "I am sure I can arrange it to be sooner. It seems I am not able to keep my hands off you, and at some point, we will be caught."

"I'm sure Juliana already knows."

"She certainly will if you go up to the house looking like that."

Emma brought her hands up to her hair, feeling the pieces that were cascading around her shoulders.

"How do you suppose you would do as a lady's maid?"

"I promise to do my very best," he said, turning her and attempting to pin the pieces back. It wasn't likely to fool anyone, but at least it was an endeavor at respectability. He lifted her bodice in place and restored her skirts to her ankles. "There. You look…"

"Thoroughly ravished?" She lifted a brow.

"Well, yes, as a matter of fact."

She sighed in exasperation. "What am I to do with you?"

"I'm not sure, but I am yours to do with what you will." They began to walk back toward the house, and Emma suddenly stopped still.

"Oh, Giles, there is something you need to know."

"What is it?" he asked, instantly on alert at the concern on her face.

"Perhaps I should let Juliana tell you—"

"Emma."

"We were going to the museum when she received a note."

"The two of you went alone to the museum after all that has happened?" He brought a hand to his temple as he felt a headache forming again, but she was waving his hand away.

"I know we likely shouldn't have, but we were very well guarded, and that is beside the point now. You need to read it, Giles. She was threatened again."

THE MYSTERY OF THE DEBONAIR DUKE

His mind was swarming with possibilities as they quickened their pace toward the house, and he pushed through the terrace doors, eager to find his sister.

"Juliana!" he called, and she stepped through the library door, her eyes widening as she looked from Giles to Emma and back again.

"Well. It seems you two have reached an understanding."

"You were right," Emma said with a sigh, as Juliana would be gloating about this for quite some time. "He does love me."

"Don't sound so chagrined," Giles teased, and when she turned to smile at him, he nearly forgot what had happened until Juliana cleared her throat.

"Where is this note?" he demanded as he caught hold of his senses once more, and Juliana started as though she had nearly forgotten. She reached into her pocket and passed it to him. His eyes ran over it quickly.

"Blast it," he muttered. "We best find Archibald. We caught the man who abducted you so it cannot be him. But he was working for someone. Someone we need to find and need to find soon. Damn it, Archibald!"

"I hardly think you can blame him," Juliana said practically, but he was already shaking his head.

"I need to speak to him. You two," he pointed at first Juliana and then Emma. "Stay here."

He caught Emma's look and added begrudgingly, "please." He managed a smile for them both. "You can start planning the wedding."

He leaned in and kissed Emma soundly.

"I'll be back."

He turned around to find his mother in the doorway. "What is—" she began.

"Juliana, please tell Mother what is happening."

And then he escaped before he had to hear anything else.

CHAPTER 25

*H*aving chosen to play the role of coward and depart before Juliana explained the new circumstances to her mother, it had been a day since Emma had seen any of the Warwick family. She was sitting in the front parlor of her parents' home, reading, when the butler stood in the doorway of the room, a rather shocked expression on his face.

"Lady Emma," he said, "the Duke of Warwick is here."

"Oh?"

She had heard a visitor arrive about an hour prior, but had assumed it was someone for her father, for he had been led into her father's study.

Suddenly she realized just what that meant.

"Oh!" she repeated. "Where is he?"

"He is in the study with your father. They would like to see you now."

"Thank you," she said, setting down her book — she had hardly registered a word as it was — before heading toward her father's study at the back of the house. Her family's townhouse was so quiet in comparison to the Warwick's grand mansion. With no siblings and her mother perpetually in her bedroom, it was Emma, her father, and the servants. Her father was most often in his study, in Parliament, or out at his clubs. It was why she spent so much time with Juliana and her family.

She knocked softly on the door before her father called her in, and she stood there in some trepidation. Her father sat behind his desk, his face a mixture of shock and relief. He had likely thought that he'd never be rid of his sole daughter and now here was a duke asking for her hand. Emma's eyes shifted across the desk to meet Giles' and she had to hide her smile behind her hand.

He was staring at her with that cheeky grin which told her he knew exactly what she was thinking. And then he winked at her and all the tension ebbed out of Emma as she knew that no matter what was to come, all was going to be fine.

"Emma," her father said, his voice stilted as he blinked while looking at her as though seeing her for the first time. "His Grace asked for your hand."

"Did he, now?" Emma said, finally returning her gaze to her father.

"He did."

"What did you say?" she asked, trying to keep the smile from spreading.

"Well…. Yes."

Giles cleared his throat. "I explained to your father that there has been some threat to my family. I believe it would be wise that we are married in a small, private ceremony. I shall go to the archbishop to try to keep any news of the marriage from the papers. The less people who know we are married, the better. I do not want you to become another pawn for someone to use against me."

Emma nodded. "I'm glad you trust I will not be a hindrance to you."

There was a lot more she had to say, but she couldn't very well do so with her father here.

"Of course not," Giles said before standing. "I'll be going now. I'd like to get that special license secured."

"Today?" Emma gasped.

"I'd like to be married as quickly as possible," he said.

Emma nodded, slightly stunned at the great change in direction her life seemed about to take. "I shall walk you out."

"Very good." He leaned over the desk and shook her father's hand. "Thank you, Lord Greenwich."

Her father nodded and Emma smiled at him. "After His Grace departs, I shall go inform Mother."

"She shall be very pleased."

Emma inclined her head. She wasn't sure if that was true, but she hoped it would cheer her mother.

She followed Giles out the door, silent as they walked down the hall. Emma was well aware that the staff would be intrigued by his visit and likely waiting behind closed doors to learn more about his intentions.

"Did you speak to Mr. Archibald?" she murmured when they stood in the foyer.

He snorted. "I just asked your father for your hand, and you are asking me about Archibald?"

She chuckled. "It's on my mind."

"There's not much he can do now," Giles said. "Except for one thing."

"Which is?"

"He's going to protect Juliana. For whatever reason, she seems to be the one who is most targeted. Perhaps she is the easiest to access. She's going to need someone with her at all times."

Emma grimaced. "Have you told her yet?"

"No," he said soberly. "I think I'll wait until after the wedding. Wouldn't want to ruin it."

"So…" She reached up and tugged on the lapels of his jacket. "When are we going to be married?"

"Tomorrow."

"Tomorrow?" She gaped at him.

"If you are prepared for it."

"I— Yes, I suppose I am. It's just so soon."

"It is. But I want you close and for more reasons than one. I am concerned, of course, that marrying me could put you in harm's way, but I promise that I will keep you safe. Do you trust me?"

"Of course I trust you," she said, not hesitating or having to think about it any further. "I love you."

"And I love you. Wife."

"Not yet!" she swatted him.

"But soon. Very soon." He leaned in as if he was going to kiss her, but then he looked beyond her and smiled. Emma heard a slight "eep!" from behind her as Giles chuckled.

"I believe we are alone now," he murmured, moving closer to her. "Besides, what is the worst that could happen? A servant catches us and tells someone, forcing us to wed?"

Emma laughed as she lifted her head and accepted his kiss.

While already looking very forward to the next one.

* * *

GILES STOOD in front of the hearth in the drawing room, his hands clasped in front of him as he waited for the love of his life to enter the room.

The room was full, although he was well aware that it was a small number of people compared to the wedding his mother had imagined for him. He wasn't entirely sure that she would ever forgive him for thwarting her, although he had promised that he would eventually hold a celebration of sorts once their family was no longer in any danger.

"She'll come around to your choice," his grandmother had told him confidently. "What difference will it make? Your Lady Emma practically lives here anyway."

That was going to take some getting used to — determining how to reconcile the girl who had been best friends with his sister throughout her life and the woman he had fallen in love with.

But he supposed that would all be determined in time. Right now, there were other things on his mind. Namely, making Emma his bride.

She stepped into the room on the arm of her father and suddenly everything else disappeared. His family sitting on the sofa, the vicar in front of the fireplace, the heavy draperies of the room, the ancestors staring down at him. For all that mattered was her.

Emma stepped into the room with a small smile on her face — one that he knew was for him, and for him alone. She took short, slow steps — the drawing room was large but it was no church aisle — as she made her way toward him. They might not be having the large ceremony at St. George's or the chapel in the country, but Giles had promised her that he would make this as romantic and meaningful as he could.

He vowed to do everything in his power to make all that he had promised her come true.

She wore a soft blue dress that brought out the color of her eyes, eyes which were fixed on his. Her hair was pulled back softly away from her face, with a few tendrils curling around her cheeks. True to who she was, there were flowers laced throughout her coiffure. Giles imagined they must be irises, although he was not entirely sure what each flower in the gardens were named. He supposed that was something he was going to have to learn.

When she reached him, she had to incline her head toward her father to remind him that he had a few responsibilities. He chuckled under his breath and then shook her father's hand before taking both of Emma's in his own. He knew that it broke with tradition, but at this point, he didn't care.

"I love you," he mouthed to her, and she did it back, even as the vicar frowned at the two of them. Emma started shaking and he realized then that she was trying to hold in laughter. It started a chuckle within him as well, and before they knew it, they were both in the fits of mirth which takes hold when it is the least opportune time.

Emma reached out and squeezed his hand — *hard* — and it was finally enough to settle the two of them.

Before he knew it, the ceremony was over, and they were leading their families out the door and into the dining room. Even Emma's mother had attended, which he knew meant a lot to her. It was the first time he had ever met her mother, who seemed quite frail and rather sickly, but she did manage a small smile for him when they were introduced. Emma told him that no one was able to diagnose her mother with any ailment, but she felt it was more an ailment of the mind or the soul instead of the body.

He was just happy she was here. He was happy they were all here. He sat back in his chair and looked around the table. It was difficult to believe that not long ago he had been trying to convince himself that Emma was all wrong for him, that they had no business being together, that she was still just a girl.

How wrong he had been.

"What are you thinking about?"

He turned to find his bride staring up at him, her nose with its few freckles crinkling at him.

"You. Us. How everything has worked out."

She chuckled lowly. "Once we both stopped being so stubborn."

"It took you long enough."

They both started at the new voice, looking over to see that Lady Winchester had joined the conversation. Emma apparently couldn't keep the mirth in anymore, and she started to laugh.

The rest of the table looked at them in surprise, the only disapproval coming from Giles' mother and Lady Hemingway, who had arrived for the occasion.

Giles leaned in, his lips coming just behind Emma's ear. He had something to say to her, and this comment was most especially *not* for his grandmother to hear.

"When do you suppose we can leave the rest of them and go upstairs?"

"Giles!"

"I have a great wish to consummate this union."

"Don't you suppose it is too late for that? We have already done that a time or two?"

He answered her by placing his hand on her thigh beneath the table. He squeezed just hard enough to cause her to jump before his fingers began trailing upward. She shot him a look, but he only grinned before continuing his quest.

Finally, she slapped her hand down on top of his, stilling it there, where he left it — for now, at least.

His patience seemed to be rewarded, for soon the breakfast broke up and he began leading her out the door of the drawing room to the staircase, having no care whatsoever for what his mother, grandmother, and sisters might think of their sudden departure. He paused in the foyer, unable to keep his hands off her any longer.

"Giles, what are you—"

But he cut off her words as he did what he had been waiting to do all morning. He placed his hands on her hips and pulled her in close, his lips coming down over hers.

She was his wife. His, for the rest of their lives. He kissed her with all the pent-up passion from deep within. Her initial moment of hesitation was soon overwhelmed by his kiss, and she lifted her hands to his neck, circling them around it as she melted into him. Her soft lips beneath his were enough to make him forget where they were, that anyone — family or servant — could walk in on them. He lowered his hands from her hips to cup her bottom when he heard a throat clear from behind him, which was enough to make him lift his head.

"Archibald," he growled. The man really had the worst timing.

"Congratulations, Your Grace," he said, a slight smile hovering on his lips. "I apologize for the intrusion. But we need to talk."

CHAPTER 26

*E*mma kept her hand quite firmly on Giles'. For one, she liked having it there. But she also had the feeling that he needed her to hold him down as she could feel the tension simmering within him. He had been quite eager to leave this drawing room and now here they were, back in it along with Juliana and Prudence, who had insisted on accompanying them when they had seen who had arrived.

"I'm just as involved as anyone," Juliana had said with arms crossed over her chest, to which Archibald had shrugged and nodded.

"She is actually more correct than she knows," he had said, a fact that didn't bode well for any of them.

"Out with it, Archibald," Giles practically barked. "We are in the middle of something."

Juliana snorted while Emma couldn't help the heat that rose in her cheeks, for more reason than simple embarrassment.

"Very well," Archibald said. "We have discovered something — or someone — that might provide us some answers."

Giles simply raised a brow.

"You recall Mrs. Lewis."

"Of course."

"Who is Mrs. Lewis?" Juliana demanded.

"A woman Father was paying for years. She would not speak to us," Giles answered, and Emma had to look down so that Juliana wouldn't see the knowledge in her eyes. Juliana might never forgive her for not telling her what she knew.

"We know now why your father was paying her," Archibald said, pausing a beat, and Emma had to wonder whether it was for dramatics. "She had a son."

Emma sucked in a breath as she realized what that meant. It took Giles and his sisters a few moments longer.

"A son?" Giles repeated.

"Yes." Archibald nodded. "If the dates of the payments are accurate, my guess is that the previous duke was likely his father."

There was a pause.

"A-are you saying that we have another brother?" Juliana asked, her voice near a squeak, and Archibald nodded.

"From what I can tell, yes."

"How old is he?" Giles asked.

"Thirty."

"The same age as I am," Giles murmured. "Where is he? And what does he want with our family?"

Archibald held up a hand. "He lives in London, works as a physician. It seems your father's money paid for some education. As for his connection to your family, I will be honest with you. I have no idea if he is even aware that his father was a duke or if he has any knowledge of you at all."

"How did you learn about him?"

"By following Mrs. Lewis and keeping an eye on her house. He visits at least once a week."

"Does he seem like a gentleman?" Prudence asked, and all eyes turned on her.

"What does that matter?" Giles asked.

"I don't know, I suppose I was just wondering if he seems like the sort who would try to kill his half-brother."

"Pru, you cannot tell from a man's countenance if he is a killer," Juliana said with some exasperation.

"I'm just saying—"

"You will question him, Archibald?" Giles demanded.

Mr. Archibald nodded. "Yes, but I think our best approach is for me to befriend him first, try to get a better understanding of who he is and what he knows."

"You really think he could have had something to do with our father's death, with Juliana's abduction, with the attempt on my life?"

Archibald let out a sigh that was hardly audible, but a sigh it was.

"I will be honest. I've never had a case like this. Most are tied up neatly in due time. This one is… convoluted."

"Have you determined the origins of the letter Juliana received at the museum?"

"Not yet."

Giles stood. "Well, then. You have work to do. Also, you will begin the other job today."

Archibald looked troubled but he nodded.

"What job is that?" Juliana asked.

Giles turned to his sister, and Emma waited as expectantly as Juliana, except that she had an inkling of what this was about. And Juliana was not going to like it.

"Jules, you seem to be the one this man is going after in order to get to our family," Giles began. "We have had Archibald's men watching you, but you need greater protection."

"So, what are you going to do?" Juliana asked, her eyes shooting fire at her brother, "keep me locked in this house?"

"No," he said, shaking his head. "Archibald here is going to personally watch over you."

Juliana's eyes quickly slid over Mr. Archibald, and Emma leaned forward when she saw the look in Juliana's eyes. She had expected Juliana to be angry, to resist the idea, but she hadn't expected to see the fear or hesitancy there. What could that possibly mean?

"That will not be necessary," Juliana said firmly, but while Emma knew Giles could be a pushover when it came to his sisters, it seemed that he was not going to be moved on this.

"It doesn't matter what you think," he said. "It is done. Until we can determine the threat, you are under Archibald's care."

"Giles!" she hissed. "We will talk about this."

"I am sure we will."

"What is happening in here?"

They all paused when his mother's figure filled the doorway and she stepped into the room hesitantly.

"Mother," Giles greeted her. "You remember Mr. Archibald."

"I do."

"He is going to be watching out for Juliana over the coming days to ensure her safety."

"Is there another threat?" she asked, looking among all of them.

"There is until we know who is behind all of this. Archibald has one idea, but he needs time to look into it."

"Will Juliana be available to go to society events?"

"Archibald and I will discuss each situation," Giles said, pausing for a moment before asking, "Mother, are there any secrets in the family? Anything we should know about?"

A fleeting edge of panic filled her expression before she quickly — too quickly — shook her head.

"No."

"Very well," he said, knowing that he couldn't push her, that she would tell him when she was ready.

Or his grandmother would. He hadn't seen her in the room until now, when she had pushed her cane forward and was using it to move her daughter out of the way so that she could see the rest of them.

"Stay vigilant," she said now. "All of you. Why, if anything happened…"

She trailed off, and Emma found her eyes watering as Prudence stood and went over to the doorway, patting her grandmother's hand. "We love you too," she said, speaking for them all.

They dispersed, and Giles took Emma's hand, leading her up the stairs, although he was not nearly as exuberant this time around.

"Are you all right?" she asked as he led her to his bedroom.

"I suppose I will be in time," he said, and Emma squeezed his hand, trying to lighten the mood.

"I have a feeling that it will be quite interesting to watch Matthew Archibald try to keep Juliana in line."

"He will have his hands full," Giles agreed. "I'm not sure how Archibald feels about minding a noblewoman, but he will be well-compensated, that is for certain."

"I am looking forward to this being behind us," Emma said. "Although I have a thought."

She took a step toward him and began slipping the buttons of his jacket through their holes, untying his cravat and taking great pleasure in that small slice of bare chest that peeked through at her.

"What is that?"

"If you wait until everything is perfect to enjoy life and be happy, you could be waiting a long time."

"What are you trying to say then?"

"I'm saying that we best be happy right now."

"I suppose I can get behind that," he murmured.

"Besides," she said with a sly grin, "you did want to consummate this marriage."

"I do."

"Then there is no time like the present."

Emma knew how much he had on his mind. Family that needed protection. A potential half-brother, illegitimate as he may be, but a half-brother, nonetheless.

So for now, in this moment, she gave herself one purpose — and that was to make him forget it all, to focus on the here and now. That much she could do for him, after all that he was giving to her.

She ran her hands down his chest, sinking to her knees in front of him, unfastening his fall and pulling it away.

"What are you doing?" he asked.

"What you did to me," she replied as he sprang free in front of her, and she reached up, stroking her hand down the velvety length of him. He let out a primitive growl that made her grin, enjoying the power she held over him. She leaned in and tentatively placed her mouth around the tip of him. When he jerked in surprise, she was no longer tentative as she began to move back and forth, testing, tasting, teasing, and finally, giving him what he really wanted. He placed his hand gently over the back of her head as she rocked forward and back with her hand on the hilt of him, covering what she couldn't take within.

Until he was finally jerking back away from her, a sheen of sweat on his forehead.

"On the bed," he grunted, and while Emma didn't ordinarily like being told what to do, his direction sent a thrill through her, and she actually did what he said. He jumped on the bed overtop of her.

"Too many clothes," he said, and together they shed the

last of them, their wedding garments now in a heap on the floor beside them, until he was gloriously naked on top of her and she was shivering with anticipation.

His fingers found her center, toying with her, delving into her just enough that he obviously realized how ready she was for him, how bringing him pleasure had surprisingly added to her own.

Then he notched against her, driving in, filling her, and she cried out in sheer joy at the sensations deep within. He rocked back and forth, at first soft and slow, and then increasing in speed and depth as he was swept away in the sensations between them — and Emma didn't care. In fact, she loved it, her hands around his back, her nails digging in as she held on and let him take her away.

The pressure within built slowly at first, until she was on the edge, waiting for sweet release. When it washed over her, she threw her head back and cried out as he came along with her, until they were both spent, lying there in awe.

"Well. That was a lovely afternoon, Your Grace," Giles said, laughter in his voice.

"I can say the same, Your Grace," she said, looking over his shoulder at his chamber around them. "Do you suppose anyone heard us?"

"Yes. But I find that I do not care."

"Perhaps we should move into the duke's quarters."

When he stilled at her suggestion, she placed a hand on his shoulder. "I could redecorate first. Make it your own."

"Our own."

"Yes, I suppose your mother might not take kindly to me ousting her from her rooms."

"She will move, because that is what she is expected to do, and my mother will always do what is expected," Giles said, his voice muffled as he was face down in the pillow, his other hand wrapped around her waist. "And you may do as you please with your own rooms — here and in the country. But at night—" he tugged her closer "—at night, you will be with me. In my bed."

"I suppose I could agree to that."

"As for the duke's rooms… yes, I suppose if you would like to redecorate, I would most appreciate it."

Emma swallowed the lump in her throat as she ran a hand over Giles' hair. He wanted to be so strong, so powerful, yet he was able to ask for help when needed. She loved that about him.

And decided to tell him so.

"I love you, Giles," she said softly.

He turned his head and looked at her, those eyes with their spark of mischief — now for her and her alone, gleaming up at her.

"I love you too."

EPILOGUE

*E*mma had her hands deep in the soil, preparing the ground for her roses. Giles had placed the various breeds she desired on special order, and they were to be arriving soon. She figured she might as well prepare for them.

A shadow cast over her, and she looked up to find Juliana standing there.

"Jules!" she said, delighted. They were as close as ever and yet… their relationship had changed. Emma couldn't quite put her finger on it, but since Juliana had found out that she and Giles had feelings for one another, there was something between them, something that hadn't been there before.

Juliana took a seat on the stone border of the garden next to her.

"Do you mind?" she asked, and Emma shook her head.

"Of course not."

Juliana was silent and Emma tried to determine what was bothering her.

"I know having Archibald follow you around is not ideal," she attempted.

"Having *anyone* follow me around is not ideal."

"At least he is handsome," Emma said, sitting back on her heels and looking at her friend, attempting levity.

"Are you supposed to say that now?" Juliana said with a small smile, tilting her head to the side.

"Just because I am married does not mean that I cannot appreciate when a man has good looks," Emma said confidently, although Juliana snorted.

"Don't let my brother hear you say that."

Emma smiled, and then looked at Juliana. "I—" she wasn't quite sure how to say it. "I want you to know how important you are to me. That you are the best friend that I could ever have, and I appreciate that you have been there for me, even as Giles and I became close. You do know that, don't you?"

Juliana looked at her with a small smile on her face. "I do. And I came here because I wanted to say that I'm sorry if I ever made you feel that you shouldn't be with him."

"To the contrary!" Emma exclaimed. "You always encouraged me to go after what I wanted. What I needed."

Juliana blinked a few times. "I don't want anything to change between us."

Emma sat next to her and took her hand in hers. "Neither do I. And I don't suppose it has to — except that I might not share, um, certain things with you that pertain to—"

Juliana held up a hand. "You do not need to say it."

They laughed together and for a moment, everything was as it was before and Emma's heart warmed.

"He loves you so much you know." Juliana said.

"I know," Emma replied. "I love him too."

"I'm glad."

They sat together in companiable silence until Emma sensed that there was more Juliana needed to talk about.

"What do you feel about this potential new brother?" Emma asked.

"Unsettled," Juliana said. "But I decided that I will wait and see what comes of it before assuming anything. Best not to worry until there is reason to."

"A wise sentiment," Emma said, bumping her shoulder against her friend's. "It will be all right, you know. Giles has hired the best, and he will do anything for you and Prudence."

"And you, too."

"I know."

They paused for a moment before Emma whispered. "I have a secret."

"Oh?" Juliana raised a brow.

"I, ah…" she looked around furtively. "I'm late."

"Late for what?"

Emma cleared her throat. "*Late.*"

Juliana frowned. "La—*oh*! Emma!" she exclaimed, as she must have realized what the timing would have been.

"You won't tell anyone, will you?" Emma asked. "Giles doesn't even know. I will tell him shortly."

"Of course," Juliana said, although her brow was still furrowed, and Emma knew why — she was doing the calculations in her head. "So when we were in the country — *Emma!*"

She looked at her with eyes round, until the two of them couldn't help it. They dissolved into laughter once more.

And everything was as it should be.

THE END

* * *

Dear reader,

While we have reached Giles and Emma's happily-ever-after, we are not exactly at "the end" of the story, as you might have guessed. There is still a rather sizeable mystery encompassing the Warwick family, a mystery that will be continued in the next story – which is that of Juliana as she attempts to navigate her life and her secret society with the addition of a bodyguard she most certainly has not asked for. We come to realize, however, that her abduction may have affected her slightly more than she lets on, so perhaps all of her protection isn't entirely for naught.

If you'd like to continue with her story, there is a preview on the pages after this one, or you can find it on Amazon: The Secret of the Dashing Detective.

If you haven't yet signed up for my newsletter, I would love to have you join us! You will receive Unmasking a Duke for free, as well as links to giveaways, sales, new releases, and stories about my coffee addiction, my struggle to keep my plants alive, and how much trouble one loveable wolf-lookalike dog can get into.

www.elliestclair.com/ellies-newsletter

Or you can join my Facebook group, Ellie St. Clair's Ever Afters, and stay in touch daily.

Until next time, happy reading!

With love,
Ellie

* * *

The Secret of the Dashing Detective
The Remingtons of the Regency
Book 2

LADY JULIANA KNOWS **she is in danger. But does she really need a bodyguard?**

One abduction and suddenly her brother, the Duke, begins treating her like a damsel in distress. Lady Juliana, however, is anything but – she is a woman who knows her own mind, and is determined to make a difference. But just how is she supposed to work for her secret society protecting animals when she is being followed around by a dashing detective?

Matthew Archibald has taken on many jobs in the past, but never did he think he would be playing nursemaid to the spoiled sister of a duke. Little does he realize, however, that there is much more to the fiery, spirited woman than he initially thought.

Matthew soon finds his focus wavering as he tries to determine just who is threatening the Remington family. But the closer he comes to Lady Juliana, the less he is able to stay professional. Will his growing feelings for her come to endanger them both?

THE SECRET OF THE DASHING
DETECTIVE - CHAPTER ONE

"*Y*ou may call it a prison, but it is certainly the loveliest prison I have ever seen."

Juliana couldn't help but laugh at her dearest friend and now sister-in-law. Emma always found a way to see the light in most situations, no matter how dire they might be.

"I suppose I am being rather dramatic," Juliana admitted, tapping her fingertips against the stone bench beneath her. "I am well aware that most people would give anything to be trapped in one of London's finest mansions."

"You are correct," Emma said diplomatically as she dug a hole in the garden bed next to Juliana's bench before pouring water into it from the pot at her side. "And yet, I understand that feeling trapped is feeling trapped, no matter what luxuries might surround you."

Juliana sighed. "You do understand me as no one else does."

Her sister, Prudence, snorted from the path she was walking around the circular flower bed, close enough that she could remain part of the conversation. "I am standing right here, Jules."

Juliana rolled her eyes good-naturedly with a smile for her elder sister.

"You know I love you as much as I love anyone, Pru, but we will never completely understand one another."

"I suppose that is true."

Juliana allowed her eyes to drift over the great expanse of gardens that composed the grounds surrounding Warwick House. It sat a few streets east of Berkley Square in the middle of London. At one point in time, it had been near the edge of the city but was now surrounded by houses, businesses and neighbourhoods. Yet it still felt like one could become lost in here, away from the crowds of most London streets.

It could also feel rather isolating.

"Giles is only trying to keep you safe, Juliana," Emma said softly.

"I know," Juliana replied. It was true – her brother *was* trying to keep her safe. Their family was clearly under threat. They had thought their father's death over a year ago had been an isolated incident, even though the physician had told them he had likely been poisoned. It was widely assumed that Juliana's brother had killed him due to the hatred between him and their father, but no one had yet legally questioned the new duke.

Just over a month ago, however, Juliana had been abducted as the kidnappers intended to draw out Giles to kill him too – and the plan had nearly worked. Fortunately, Giles had only been grazed by the bullet.

"Here we thought we would be done with all of this after Mr. Archibald found the man that kidnapped you," Prudence said, drawing Emma's ire when she snapped a flower off of a bush and began to pick the pedals off one at a time. Juliana knew she would be chanting the "loves me not" rhyme, even though Prudence didn't have potential suitors – nor, apparently, did she wish for any.

"We should have known it would be much more complicated than that," Emma murmured as she gently picked up a small sapling and placed it in the hole before pushing dirt around it.

"I shall never understand why a duchess sits in the dirt and plants herself," Prudence said, her nose wrinkling as she watched Emma, who simply laughed at her.

"First, I only became a duchess two weeks ago, and I enjoyed such work long before that," Emma said. "Secondly, there is nothing that fills my soul like sitting in the gardens or the orangery and working with plants. You should try it."

"No, thank you," Prudence said politely as she continued her slow stroll.

"Why, do you have too much else to do?" Juliana asked, raising an eyebrow, and Prudence eyed her with a withering glare.

"Who are you to be asking me such a thing?"

"I have much to do," Juliana said indignantly, sitting up straight on the bench now. "My work is important."

Prudence clasped her hands behind her back.

"I know it was important to you, Jules, but Giles will never allow you to go back."

Juliana stared at her mutinously. "We shall see about that."

"Perhaps once we have this threat negated," Emma began diplomatically, but Juliana stopped her words.

"You are married to my brother now, Emma, which is wonderful and I am so happy we are now sisters and actually live together, but really, how would you like being kept under lock and key and told where you can go and who you can see?"

"You do not have to remain here," Emma said, moving

onto the next hole. "You are welcome to leave, which means that you are not a true prisoner."

"I can leave, but only if I am accompanied by Mr. Archibald."

"Yes," Emma conceded, rising to her feet and brushing dirt off the knees of the morning gown she had ruined long ago but kept for activities such as these. "He is not so horrible, though, now is he? Rather pleasant to look at, I believe you said at one point in time."

"He will report everything to Giles," Juliana grumbled, crossing her arms over her chest. Her brother had initially hired Matthew Archibald to determine who had killed their father – or to at least make it look like he was trying to come to some conclusion, for at the time, Giles could have cared less who had taken their father out of this world. When Juliana had been taken, however, Mr. Archibald had helped the family to recover her. Since then, the detective had been attempting to determine who was behind the scheme while also keeping the family safe.

"It is not as though you do anything disreputable," Prudence added in.

"No," Juliana said, taking off her bonnet and setting it next to her as she raised her face to the sun, waving away Prudence's warning regarding her freckles. "But there are some activities I take part in that Giles wouldn't exactly be... pleased about."

"Activities that he has forbidden?" Emma asked, looking over at her now, and Juliana heaved a dramatic sigh.

"It doesn't make any sense whatsoever, Emma. Even you must admit that. Mrs. Stone is a lovely woman and there is no reason to keep me from my work. We are not harming anyone. In fact, we are doing the exact opposite."

"I think it is more so that he is worried about what might

happen to you if you continue to take a stand for what you believe in."

"You sound like my mother now," Juliana said, chewing on her thumbnail.

"Oh, Jules, I am sorry," Emma said, walking over to her now. She lifted a hand to place it on Juliana's arm but stopped when they both looked down and saw how dirty it was. "You know I love you more than anything."

"I do," Juliana said with a nod and a smile, for she knew what Emma said was true.

"Good," Emma said, relief evident on her face. Their friendship hadn't been quite as strong and sure since Emma and Giles had married. "Now, do tell us, how is everything with Lord Hemingway?"

"Lord Hemingway?" Juliana asked with some surprise. She hadn't even considered the man as they sat in the afternoon sun, for she had been intent on how to return to her work despite Giles having forbid it. "He is…" she tried to think of the right words to describe the man her mother was encouraging her to accept. "He is my father's cousin son."

"Obviously," Prudence said with a snort.

"And he is…"

She scratched her nose.

"Boring?" Prudence supplied, and Juliana opened her mouth to refute her, but found it impossible to do so directly.

"He is nice."

"Nice?" Prudence repeated. "Nice is what you use to describe something that you have nothing bad to say about, but nothing particularly good either."

"I do not know him well," Juliana said defensively. "He has visited with us before, of course, when he has accompanied his mother, and he did call upon us in order to request a potential courtship, but we have not yet had the opportunity to spend much time together."

"How interesting it would be with Mr. Archibald following you around," Emma said, unable to hold back her laughter, to which Juliana could only sigh, wondering what that would look like.

The truth – one that she hadn't shared even with Emma – was that Prudence was right. Lord Hemingway was rather boring, even if he was everything she had thought she had wanted – a man she could tolerate, who would allow her to live her the life she chose. At least, she assumed he would. He didn't exactly seem to be a man of strong opinions, not with a mother like his. But she also wasn't entirely sure she was prepared for anything unpredictable. Not any more. She'd had enough surprises already, and her other secret was just how much her abduction had affected her. Boring and predictable? She didn't have much issue with that at the moment.

"Now," Emma said, "the question is, how are you going to handle Mr. Archibald?"

~~~~~

Matthew Archibald drummed his fingers on the desk in front of him, leaning back as he surveyed the room. His offices were small, located in the front of a tall brick building in the midst of Holborn. It was a respectable enough location that his higher-class clients felt comfortable in meeting him here, while it wasn't so high up that those who hired him from his own social status were not too intimidated to seek him out.

Currently the room in front of him was filled with the men who worked for him, the ones he could trust implicitly. He was currently failing at the most important job he had ever acquired, and he needed all of the help he could get.

The men were at ease, some sitting on the chairs they had assembled from various corners of the room, some on the other desks that were available for use when needed. Others were leaning against the wall, in relaxed poses. Matthew couldn't help a small smile for those he had gathered. They were good men, hard-working, reliable.

And he was letting them down.

He cleared his throat to capture their attention, and the ten men in the room immediately quieted down and turned to him.

Matthew inclined his head, signaling one man to come to the front with him. Owen Green had not only been his closest of friends since they were boys, but he had been the one to begin this operation with him all those years ago, and he had remained by his side ever since. On the days Matthew wished he had two of himself, Owen became that second person for him.

"Listen up, men," he said, as shocked as he had always been at how many now worked for him. Theirs had been a slow build to their current size, but he appreciated the trust of each and every one of them. "You know that we have had some difficulty in watching over the duke and his family. After Lady Juliana's abduction, we vowed to keep the family safe, and yet someone was able to enter their premises of the country house just outside Watford. We returned to London as it would be easier to watch over them all at Warwick House. It is, of course, large itself, but not nearly as sprawling as Remington House in the country."

They were all watching him, heads nodding. None of this was news, and they had all taken their turns guarding the houses and the family.

"Thus far, we have kept them safe here in London. That is

because of you and I thank you for that. But it is more important than ever for us to determine who is threatening them so that we can finish this job. The duke will not continue to pay us forever."

He saw some glances of unease between the men now. Up until now, most of their jobs had come to a fairly swift conclusion. But then, most were not particularly complicated. A husband getting cuckolded, a theft that was so obvious that Matthew wondered how the victim didn't determine the culprit himself.

"What you do not know is that we have uncovered a secret from the previous duke's past. He had an illegitimate son with a woman by the name of Mrs. Lewis. She used to live in the village near the duke's country seat but moved to London some years ago, likely to accompany her son when he came to school here. The duke had been paying her – perhaps blackmail? – until about five years ago. We have located the man and I am going to make contact with him to determine what he knows and what ill will he could hold toward the family."

"How will you do that?" one man, Pip, asked from the back.

"I'm going to establish a friendship," Matthew said. "It will be much easier to draw him out that way than attempt to force information out of a man."

Much more palatable, that was. He had tried both ways before and always struggled with the latter.

"Do we have any other suspects?" another man, Anderson, asked him now, and Matthew tapped his fingers on the desk again as he let Owen answer, for he had been the one keeping an eye on his other suspect.

"We cannot forget about Lord Hemingway, simply because he is the one who would gain the title if anything were to happen to the duke," Owen said. "But the man is as clean as they come. Has never even cheated at gambling from what I can tell. No one has a bad word to say about him. He's just a good man, if a bit under his mother's thumb. He is interested in courting the Lady Juliana, so he will remain part of the family, if nothing else."

"Keep an eye on him, just in case," Matthew said, wondering why he felt that instinctual turn of his stomach when Owen spoke of Hemingway's interest in Lady Juliana. What did it matter to him if the two got together?

"I will."

"While I attempt to befriend Lewis, I will not be able to watch him at other times, for the duke has requested that I remain available to ensure Lady Juliana's safety," Matthew continued. "She received a threatening note when out at the museum not long ago and the duke is concerned that she has been targeted as the weakest point in the family. So Mouse, you will also watch over Lewis, see what else he is up to. Good?"

"Good."

"The rest of you will continue your shifts watching over the family as we have discussed. Then we have the few of you who are on the Sheffield case."

He moved the discussion over to the smaller case, while his mind remained on the Warwick threat. He was missing something, he knew it, he thought, rubbing his chin as a piece of information poked at the back of his mind but didn't quite make it through.

Just what was it?

KEEP READING The Secret of the Dashing Detective!

ALSO BY ELLIE ST. CLAIR

The Remingtons of the Regency
The Mystery of the Debonair Duke
The Secret of the Dashing Detective
The Clue of the Brilliant Bastard
The Quest of the Reclusive Rogue

Reckless Rogues
The Earls's Secret
The Viscount's Code
Prequel, The Duke's Treasure, available in:
I Like Big Dukes and I Cannot Lie

The Unconventional Ladies
Lady of Mystery
Lady of Fortune
Lady of Providence
Lady of Charade

The Unconventional Ladies Box Set

To the Time of the Highlanders
A Time to Wed
A Time to Love
A Time to Dream

Thieves of Desire

The Art of Stealing a Duke's Heart

A Jewel for the Taking

A Prize Worth Fighting For

Gambling for the Lost Lord's Love

Romance of a Robbery

Thieves of Desire Box Set

The Bluestocking Scandals

Designs on a Duke

Inventing the Viscount

Discovering the Baron

The Valet Experiment

Writing the Rake

Risking the Detective

A Noble Excavation

A Gentleman of Mystery

The Bluestocking Scandals Box Set: Books 1-4

The Bluestocking Scandals Box Set: Books 5-8

Blooming Brides

A Duke for Daisy

A Marquess for Marigold

An Earl for Iris

A Viscount for Violet

The Blooming Brides Box Set: Books 1-4

Happily Ever After

The Duke She Wished For

Someday Her Duke Will Come

Once Upon a Duke's Dream

He's a Duke, But I Love Him

Loved by the Viscount

Because the Earl Loved Me

Happily Ever After Box Set Books 1-3

Happily Ever After Box Set Books 4-6

The Victorian Highlanders

Duncan's Christmas - (prequel)

<u>Callum's Vow</u>

<u>Finlay's Duty</u>

<u>Adam's Call</u>

<u>Roderick's Purpose</u>

<u>Peggy's Love</u>

<u>The Victorian Highlanders Box Set Books 1-5</u>

Searching Hearts

Duke of Christmas (prequel)

Quest of Honor

Clue of Affection

Hearts of Trust

Hope of Romance

Promise of Redemption

Searching Hearts Box Set (Books 1-5)

Christmas

Christmastide with His Countess

Her Christmas Wish

Merry Misrule

A Match Made at Christmas

A Match Made in Winter

Standalones

Always Your Love

The Stormswept Stowaway

A Touch of Temptation

For a full list of all of Ellie's books, please see
www.elliestclair.com/books.

ABOUT THE AUTHOR

Ellie has always loved reading, writing, and history. For many years she has written short stories, non-fiction, and has worked on her true love and passion -- romance novels.

In every era there is the chance for romance, and Ellie enjoys exploring many different time periods, cultures, and geographic locations. No matter when or where, love can always prevail. She has a particular soft spot for the bad boys of history, and loves a strong heroine in her stories.

Ellie and her husband love nothing more than spending time at home with their children and Husky cross. Ellie can typically be found at the lake in the summer, pushing the stroller all year round, and, of course, with her computer in her lap or a book in hand.

She also loves corresponding with readers, so be sure to contact her!

www.elliestclair.com
ellie@elliestclair.com

Ellie St. Clair's Ever Afters Facebook Group

Made in United States
Orlando, FL
02 March 2024

44332066R00146